THE DEVIL'S SWORD

Douglas E. Richards

D1416913

Paragon Press

Copyright © 2009 by Douglas E. Richards

Published by Paragon Press, 2010
ParagonPressSF@gmail.com

ISBN: 978-0-9826184-3-1

Library of Congress Control Number: 2010928543

Printed in the United States of America

First Edition

ABOUT THE AUTHOR

Douglas E. Richards is the *New York Times* and *USA Today* bestselling author of *WIRED*, its sequel, *AMPED,* and the new standalone sci-fi/technothriller, *THE CURE.* He has also written six middle grade/young adult novels widely acclaimed for their appeal to boys, girls, and adults alike. In 2010, in recognition of his work, he was selected to be a "special guest" at San Diego Comic-Con International, along with such icons as Stan Lee, Ray Bradbury, and Rick Riordan. Douglas currently lives in San Diego, California, with his wife, two children, and two dogs.

ALSO BY DOUGLAS E RICHARDS

WIRED (Adult science fiction/technothriller)

AMPED (The WIRED Sequel)

THE CURE (Standalone sci-fi/technothriller)

Middle Grade/YA

The Prometheus Project: Trapped (Book 1)

The Prometheus Project: Captured (Book 2)

The Prometheus Project: Stranded (Book 3)

The Devil's Sword

Ethan Pritcher, Body Switcher

Out of This World

To my son, Ryan, who fell in love with fencing, thereby introducing me to this fantastic sport and the wonderful community of fencers. Without you, and without having the opportunity to accompany you to a tournament on a military base, this book would never have been written. I am proud of the numerous trophies you were able to win, but even prouder of the sportsmanship, friendship, determination, and leadership you so consistently displayed along the way.

THE DEVIL'S SWORD

Douglas E. Richards

Paragon Presss

PART ONE

"Those who play with the devil's toys will be brought by degrees to wield his sword."

　　—R. Bucminster Fuller,
　　　American Author, Architect, and Inventor

Note: All quotes in this book are taken from "The Notebook of Cool Quotes," compiled by Kevin Taylor.

CHAPTER 1

"If someone comes at you with a sword, run if you can. Kung Fu doesn't always work."

—Bruce Lee, Martial Arts Expert, Actor

Kevin Taylor drove the tip of his sword into Ben Chang's chest with a ferocious lunge. He moved with the blinding quickness of a striking cobra, and his attack took Ben completely by surprise, impaling him before he could even begin to react.

Kevin shook his fist triumphantly. *Yesssss* he thought excitedly to himself. He *loved* stabbing people.

"The attack is from my left," announced the referee. "Attack arrives. Touch for Taylor. Taylor leads seven touches to four."

Ben Chang groaned miserably. His friend had set a trap for him and he had walked straight into it.

Kevin Taylor's white, padded, outer clothing was soaked in sweat, and he was breathing hard now, even between points. A black, steel-mesh helmet enveloped his entire head like an enormous dragonfly eye that had erupted from his shoulders. He pulled the heavy mask off, wiped sweat from his eyes with the back of his gloved right hand, and replaced the mask. Once again, his face vanished behind the tight black mesh.

"*On guard!*" said the referee. "Fencer's ready. *Fence!*"

A crowd of about twenty spectators stood along one side of the fencing strip; a metal pathway laid out on the floor like a gleaming silver sidewalk, six feet wide and forty-six feet long. The two boys moved toward each other from their *on guard* lines, located about seven feet from the middle of the strip on either side. Several in the small crowd rooted loudly for one or the other of the two battling fourteen-year olds. The boys paid no attention. They were so focused on reacting to every movement of the other's sword an alien spaceship could have landed next to them and they wouldn't have noticed.

Kevin and Ben raced up and down the long metal strip, lunging, retreating and crossing swords. They never faced each other full on, but rather were turned sideways in the stance used by swordfighters throughout history to expose as little of their bodies to the enemy's blade as possible. The front foot of each fencer was extended forward and pointed toward the other while the back foot of each was well behind them, at a ninety-degree angle to their lead foot. Their knees were bent and they stayed balanced, ready to accelerate explosively into an attack or rocket themselves backwards in retreat with equal agility.

Kevin began an attack that was blocked; the boys' blades crashing against each other with an unmistakable metal clang. The instant Ben pushed Kevin's blade aside he went in for the kill, but Kevin spun away from his friend's thrust and flicked his sword at Ben like a whip. Instead of striking Ben's torso, the tip of Kevin's blade hit his friend's arm. Ben winced in pain. Even though the material covering his arm was thick, the sword-turnedwhip bit into his flesh and he felt a sharp sting that was in no hurry to go away.

"*Halt!*" shouted the referee as Ben tried to rub the pain from his arm. "The initial attack is from my left," he announced. "The attack is parried. Riposte from my right is 'no'. Counterattack from my left is off target. No touch. Score remains seven touches to four." The fencers quickly returned to the ready position. "Fencer's ready," said the referee. *"Fence!"*

During the brief break in the action, Kevin had glanced at the electronic scoring display on the wall. Five seconds were left in the three-minute period. Ben had noticed this as well, and neither boy initiated any further attacks while they waited for the glowing red numbers on the display to tick down to zero.

"The second period is over," announced the ref. "There will be a one minute break followed by the third and final period."

Kevin pulled off his helmet and retreated to his end of the strip. He shot a quick glance at Rachel Felder, a fifteen-year-old girl who was close friends with both combatants, and nodded. Rachel was a fantastic fencer in her own right.

One more period to go, thought Kevin. Just three more minutes. The gold medal was so close he could almost taste it! He vowed to fence for the next three minutes as if his life depended on it.

He had no way of knowing, of course, that in just six weeks time his life really *would* depend on his fencing abilities—as would the lives of others very close to him.

CHAPTER 2

"In war, there is no second prize for runner-up."
—General Omar Bradley,
Field Commander (WW II)

John Anderson landed the small helicopter at the edge of an oval clearing in the vast woods, beside a similar chopper. Night was just falling. Other than the two men he had come to meet he doubted there was another human for twenty miles. John was a high-ranking member of an American Black Operations group, a shadowy organization whose very existence was denied by the military. He took a deep breath and stepped from the helicopter into the clearing.

"What took you so long, my friend," bellowed Diego Martinez from twenty yards away, standing at the opposite edge of the large clearing. John had never met the man in person but his deep voice was unmistakable. And while he couldn't see Diego clearly in the twilight, he could tell he was tall, thin and clean cut. Diego had once been a member of an elite unit in the Cuban army before he had teamed up with Klaus, the shorter, more muscular German standing next to him. Both men were in their thirties, extremely fit, and experts at disguise. And while English was not a first language for either of them, both spoke it perfectly; only their accents revealing their origins.

In a single, fluid motion, John turned, pulled a submachine gun from the floor of the helicopter, and came up firing, spraying both men with bullets. Fifteen rounds exploded from the barrel of the submachine gun each second, accompanied by billowing smoke and a thunderous sound that reverberated throughout the forest— as instantly recognizable as it was deafening. Small animals of every kind fled through the underbrush, and bark flew through the air as stray bullets imbedded themselves in surrounding trees.

John continued firing long past the time at which both men were surely dead. Despite the distance, they never had a chance. They had been cut down without making a single move to escape.

John rushed forward to inspect his work, but he knew what he would find. They would each have so many holes in them they would look more like bloody Swiss cheese than men.

He was ten yards away when his heart skipped a beat. Something was very wrong! After two more steps he realized what it was— his targets had not been human! Instead, they had been manikins, made up to look exactly like Diego and Klaus.

John's stomach dropped in horror and he wheeled around just as a bullet tore through his forearm, shattering bone and sending his gun flying.

John screamed in agony.

They had fooled him completely! The manikins had been convincing from a distance and in the weak light. Diego must have used a microphone to transmit his voice from the dummy, enhancing the illusion. John ripped material from his shirt and clumsily attempted to tie it around his wounded right arm, his teeth clenched in pain.

Diego lowered the assault rifle he had used to pierce John's arm and he and Klaus approached the Black Ops agent. Diego's eyes were cold, gray, and unblinking—like those of a snake trying to hypnotize its prey. "John . . . John . . . John," he said slowly, shaking his head. "Why do I get the feeling you were trying to double-cross us?"

"We can't help but be disappointed," added Klaus, his massive biceps stretching the thin material of the black t-shirt he was wearing. "We've been paying you a small fortune for information, and just when you finally know something big you turn on us."

Without warning Diego slammed the butt of his rifle into John's wounded arm, sending him reeling. He became so dizzy from the pain he fell to his knees.

"But don't worry," said Diego with a cruel smile. "You'll have plenty of chance to make it up to us."

The woods were eerily silent. John shot a quick glance to the sky in the direction from which he had arrived.

Rapid though it was, Klaus caught the movement of John's eyes. "Expecting company?" he said mockingly. "Well I'm afraid there's been a change of plans. Your back-up crew had to cancel," he finished, quite pleased with himself.

John's eyes widened in panic. "But how?" he said in disbelief. "How could you know I would try to kill you? How could you know about my back-up plan? *That's impossible!*"

"Haven't you heard," said the tall Cuban smugly. "We're the best there is."

Diego leaned forward menacingly. "Now tell us about the weapon called *The Devil's Sword.*"

CHAPTER 3

"Success is not the key to happiness. Happiness is the key to success. If you love what you are doing, you will be successful."

—Albert Schweitzer,
Winner of Nobel Peace Prize

Two Years Earlier

Kevin Taylor was a natural athlete. There was only one problem: he didn't like sports. Not any of them.

This might not have been such a huge problem in some households. But in the Taylor family, it was *unheard* of.

Kevin's father was crazy about sports. So were his two older brothers, Daniel and Cameron. Dan was two years older than Kevin and Cameron was four years older. Over the years Mr. Taylor had tried to interest his youngest son in baseball and basketball and football and ten-nis—all sports Kevin's father had played as a kid. Kevin was good at all of them, and had interest in none.

His father had never been more baffled by anything in his life. He could understand a boy not wanting to play sports if he was *horrible* at them. But a boy as athletic as Kevin not liking them went against the natural order of things. If Kevin didn't like the taste of chocolate or ice cream, this would have been hard to believe. If he hated puppies, this would have been extremely odd and troubling. *But not liking sports? Unimaginable!*

His father thought sports were so important, in fact, that about once every year he would push Kevin to continue trying them, hoping his youngest son would find one he liked. Mr. Taylor was convinced there were three critical components to living a healthy, happy, and well-balanced life—the intellectual, the social, and the physical. By this, he explained to Kevin, he meant exercising the brain, getting along with other people, and exercising the body.

When Kevin pointed out that it was possible to exercise without playing a sport, his father would go on and on about how exercise was only the beginning of the benefits of playing a sport. Sports built self-confidence. Playing a sport would help Kevin learn important lessons about teamwork. About pushing himself to his limits. About doing his best in pressure situations.

Every year Kevin and his father had the same discussion, and every year Kevin agreed to dutifully keep trying additional sports. And he did. But he continued not to have a passion for any of them. Most sports involved catching, throwing, or chasing a ball, which all seemed like pointless activities to Kevin.

Finally, on Kevin's twelfth birthday, his father gave up. He was running out of sports for his youngest son to try, and he had become convinced Kevin wouldn't be enthusiastic about any of them anyway. While Mr. Taylor truly believed the benefits of participating in sports were huge, Kevin was a great kid, and if he never found a sport he liked this was just the way it would have to be.

You can lead a horse to water, but you can't make him drink. Mr. Taylor finally decided that this particular horse would never be thirsty, and that it was time to stop leading him to water already.

CHAPTER 4

"If you're going through hell, keep going."
—Winston Churchill, British Prime Minister
Public School Fencing Champion (Foil)

Kevin's twelfth birthday came and went—and still, he was barely five feet tall. His green eyes matched those of his mother, and his face was a handsome blend of his mother's soft features and his father's more angular ones. But it was becoming clear he was taking after his short mother in the height department. His brothers, on the other hand, continued to shoot up like beanstalks and would match or exceed the height of their six-foottall father

It just wasn't fair!

Kevin was taunted and teased unmercifully by his brothers, whose favorite theme was that he was really a girl. How else to explain his disinterest in sports. They would say things like, "Cheer up Kevin. You know that you're Mom and Dad's favorite daughter," or "the leader of your Girl Scout troop called and said you need to sell more cookies."

Their second favorite theme was that Kevin was the ultimate geek. After all, he was shy, got A's in every class, and spent endless hours on his computer playing complicated war games. What more evidence of geek-hood was needed? "If you look up the definition of 'Geek' in the dictionary," they would say to Kevin, "it has your picture."

Kevin fought back, calling them "poodles", because, like dogs, all they wanted to do was catch and chase balls all day. Which might make them big shots in high school but would get them nowhere as adults. Kevin would say things like, "when you're in your thirties, wouldn't it be cool if you both worked at the same McDonald's?"

But even though he returned their teasing blow for blow, in his heart Kevin couldn't help but feel inferior to Dan and Cameron. They were stars of their sports teams. They were outgoing and had armies of friends. They were confident. *Tall*.

Kevin, on the other hand, in addition to being one of the shortest boys in his class, had a mouth full of braces. He was self-conscious and hated to be the center of attention. He never had more than one or two close friends, and spent almost all of his free time on the computer or reading about history or the military. And unlike his brothers, he felt far more comfortable alone than in a crowd.

Maybe his brothers *were* right. Maybe he *was* the ultimate geek.

Only a few months after Kevin turned twelve he made a huge mistake. When his brothers teased him about his height, instead of attacking back, he let them see it bothered him. He might as well have waved a red cape at a bull, or thrown a hunk of fresh meat into a stream filled with starving piranha. Now, in addition to taunting him about being a girl and a geek, his brothers had started calling him *runt* whenever his parents weren't around.

Kevin decided he wasn't too thrilled about being twelve. It was going to be a long, long year.

One Saturday morning, as summer approached, Kevin's mother dropped a glossy brochure next to him as he was eating breakfast at their kitchen table. "Horizons Summer Camp," was printed in bold block lettering on the cover of the brochure.

"What's this?" he said, not bothering to open the brochure. Instead, he continued to shovel massive spoonfuls of cereal into his mouth at a furious pace. He had just awoken and his short, light-brown hair was spread out haphazardly on top of his head.

"A new summer program," said his mother as she pulled out a chair and took a seat across from him, ignoring the milk running down her son's chin. "They're offering all kinds of really fun classes. At the high school. I want you to choose a few."

Kevin eyed his mother suspiciously. "Did you actually use the words *really fun* and *classes* together?" he said in disbelief. Kevin had been looking forward to building elaborate models, going to the beach, and playing war games on his computer all summer. After an entire year of school, the word *class* had a scary ring to it.

"Amusement parks are really fun," he pointed out to his mother. "Swimming is really fun." He shook his head. "Classes might be interesting—sometimes—but they're definitely *not* really fun."

"These are," said his mother, unperturbed. "Take a look. They have chess, movie-making, rocketry, fencing—"

"Fencing?" interrupted Kevin with a gleam in his eye. "You mean like sword fighting?"

His mother nodded. "Yeah, that's right. You get dressed up in protective gear and stab each other."

Kevin was instantly intrigued. He had pretended to sword fight all the time when he was younger, using everything from plastic light sabers to the cardboard tubes found inside giant rolls of wrapping paper. What kid hadn't?

Kevin swallowed yet another mouthful of cereal and raised his eyebrows. "I think I'll give that a try," he said.

Maybe his mom was right after all, he thought. This class did sound fun. And when his brothers picked on him—or whenever he was in a really bad mood and angry over the unfairness of life— being able to stab someone repeatedly seemed awfully appealing.

CHAPTER 5

"Mankind must put an end to war, or war will put an end to mankind.

—John F. Kennedy, US President

The Present

John Anderson dragged himself across several feet of forest floor and propped his back against the thick trunk of a giant oak tree at the edge of the clearing. Despite his makeshift bandage he was losing blood rapidly and even this minor exertion made him dizzy. The pain from his shattered arm was nearly overwhelming. "The Devil's Sword?" he repeated. "I have no idea what you're talking about."

Diego laughed. "I admire your patriotism, John. I really do. Klaus and I knew from the start you were only pretending to spy for us. That you were still loyal to the United States." He paused. "We knew if we ever let you get close enough to take us out, you would try to do so."

John glared at the two men hatefully. "You two are responsible for thousands of deaths," he said bitterly. "You have to be stopped."

Diego and Klaus were arms dealers, specializing in long-range missile technology. They had teamed up five years earlier and their partnership had flourished. They were now millionaires many times over. Acquiring advanced weaponry by any means possible and selling it to dictators and terrorists around the world was very good business.

Klaus laughed. "We're honored to be on your government's most wanted list. But let me assure you we will never be caught or killed. We're far too smart and resourceful."

"So let's get back to The Devil's Sword, shall we," said Diego pleasantly. "Here is what we know. Three months ago, your government secretly launched a satellite containing a missile defense system called 'Heaven's Shield'. It's based on a major breakthrough in laser technology." He paused. "We also know that it's been secretly tested and has performed brilliantly, shooting down long range ballistic missiles with one hundred percent effectiveness."

"You can see why this would interest us, right Johnny?" added Klaus. "I mean we sell long range missile technology. If the Americans can now shoot missiles out of the sky, no one will want to buy from us."

John felt weak and closed his eyes.

Diego kicked him savagely in the chest, slamming him back against the tree trunk. "You really need to pay more attention, John," hissed the Cuban. "This is important."

Diego waited patiently for John to regain his senses and then continued as if nothing had happened. "To build Heaven's Shield, your scientists needed to make huge leaps forward in laser technology. And they did. From what I understand, the system is powerful enough to reach down from space and destroy missiles as low as ninety miles above the ground." Since ballistic missiles routinely reached altitudes far higher than this in their flight paths, this would give the system plenty of room for error.

"Now there are rumors," continued Diego, "that the genius running the show stumbled onto a major discovery just before the satellite was launched. He found a way to boost the laser's power a hundred-fold. To turn this Heaven's Shield into a *weapon*—one with the power to reach all the way down to Earth."

A cool, twilight breeze rustled leaves and sent a chill through John's body. John gritted his teeth from the relentless pain and forced himself to remain as calm as possible. His only chance was if his Black Operations group began to wonder why it was taking him so long to report back and came looking for him. But even if they did, they would have little hope of finding him in time.

"We all know a weapon like this would be a gamechanger," continued Diego. "The beam could take out buildings or it could be spread out to systematically destroy entire cities. This in itself isn't so special," he noted. "Other weapons can destroy cities. What makes this one so intriguing is that it would have pinpoint accuracy. And it would be impossible to defend against. Forget about buildings. This weapon could reach out and destroy *individuals* at will, without otherwise disturbing as much as a single blade of grass."

Diego grinned, like a kid talking about a new, favorite toy. "Anyone that could be seen with a spy satellite could be vaporized instantly. It would be like those beams shot from the giant tripods in the *War of the Worlds* movie. Except worse. Far worse. This beam would originate in space and could hit anywhere, at any time. There would be no avoiding it. And worst of all, no warning. One minute you're minding your own business." He snapped his fingers. "The next you're nothing but ashes."

"It's easy to see why your agency code-named this weapon *The Devil's Sword*," said Klaus. "It would truly be an unstoppable sword of death stabbing down from space."

Diego turned to his partner and raised his eyebrows. "I had no idea you were so poetic, my friend," he said in amusement.

"Me either," said Klaus with a grin. "I just find this imagery strangely appealing." The German turned toward John and his expression hardened. "So that's what *we* know. Now it's your turn, John. Tell us what *you* know."

"What makes you think I know anything?"

"We have a number of highly placed sources in the government and military," replied Diego. "They don't know anything about this other than the rumors, but they're all convinced that *you* do. We didn't lure you here by accident, my friend. We went to a lot of trouble, in fact." He grinned. "Those manikins were expensive."

"Well you've wasted your time," spat John defiantly, wincing in pain as he did so. "Because your sources were wrong. I don't know what you're talking about. And even if did, I'd never tell you. You're going to kill me anyway, no matter what I do. At least I'll go to my grave knowing I haven't betrayed my country."

Diego laughed. "I don't doubt it, John. You're quite the hero type. But it's not just *you* we're talking about here, is it?" He pulled several three-by-five photographs from his pocket. "You have two sisters, correct? Sandra and Pamela. And they each have two children."

He tossed the photographs in John's lap and waited patiently. John almost vomited when he saw pictures of his sisters, nieces, and nephews going about their daily lives. For these two monsters to have taken photos of his family members, they must have already been within striking distance of each one of them.

"They look like a nice bunch," said Diego. "I'd sure hate for anything *bad* to happen to them," he growled threateningly. "So I'm going to let you reconsider. Their lives are in *your* hands." The tall Cuban glared at John with cold, gray eyes. "Tell us what you know. This is the last time we're going to ask," he finished icily.

CHAPTER 6

"The pen is mightier than the sword if the sword
is very short, and the pen is very sharp."
—Terry Pratchett, English Writer

Eighteen Months Earlier

Kevin loved fencing. He loved everything about it. He couldn't
wait to get to class every day and learn more. He had thought it
would be simple—just stab at your opponent—but it was anything but. Not only was it astonishingly complex, there seemed to
be an endless array of strategies and moves to learn.

When the summer class was over, he pleaded with his mother
to let him continue fencing. There were six or seven clubs in his
hometown of San Diego. Luckily, the *Excalibur Fencing Club* had
just opened and was ten minutes from his house.

Kevin went every day for three or four hours at a time until the
summer ended. Once school started, he would hurriedly finish his
homework so he could get in a few hours of fencing after dinner.
This was a time when there weren't any classes, just open fencing.
Whoever was there would practice with each other.

Kevin's mother usually just dropped him off and left, but a few
times he caught her peering into the fencing room from the doorway, watching him. His father asked him about his fencing every

once in a while but only seemed mildly interested and never came to watch.

His brothers wasted no time in adding fencing to the list of things they teased him about. They took to calling him Luke Skywalker, or Zorro, or Jack Sparrow, or the name of anyone and everyone who had ever been in a sword fighting movie, except they would insert the word "little," before the name.

Little Jack Sparrow. *Little* Zorro.

Dan especially liked calling him Yoda since, as Dan loved to point out, the green alien was a sword fighter *and* a runt—just like Kevin. Besides, he loved doing the Yoda voice.

"Yeees, yeees," said Dan one day, Yoda-style, about four months after Kevin had begun to fence. "Heard you were a boy, I have. But certain that you are actually a little girl, I have become."

"What would you know about girls, anyway, Dan?" Kevin shot back. "From what I can see, no girl will get within a mile of you."

Cameron laughed out loud, and Kevin could tell from the enraged look in Dan's eye he had hit a nerve. Especially since Dan's face had recently erupted into a red, volcano-field of acne that he was extremely self-conscious about.

"Ouch," said Cam. "That's gotta hurt, Dan."

"Shut up, *Nancy!*" Dan yelled at Kevin, deciding to stick with the, 'my little brother is actually a girl' theme for the thousandth time. "Why don't you take off your *dress,* put on your pretty white fencing outfit, and go stab someone."

"You're a moron, Dan, you know that!" said Kevin. "Stop making fun of my sport! I don't make fun of yours."

Dan rolled his eyes. "Did you just call fencing 'your sport'?" he said in disbelief. "And you call *me* a moron. Fencing is about as much a sport as ballet dancing."

"It is too a sport!" said Kevin.

"No, Dan's right," Cam chimed in. "Even your little fencing club doesn't think so. I saw one of their fliers you brought home that said, 'learn the *art* of fencing'. It's an *art*, not a *sport*."

"That's just a figure of speech," snapped Kevin.

Dan shook his head. "No it isn't. You don't have any games. You just clang your silly swords together a bunch of times and then try to stab each other. We've all done it when we were little. You just wave your arms around. You don't get any exercise and you never actually compete at *anything*."

"Not true!" insisted Kevin. "Every bout is a competition. And there are tournaments," he added adamantly.

Dan shook his head. "Kevin, why do you think Dad never comes to watch you wave your little sword?" he said with a look of exaggerated pity. "After all, he comes to Cam's and my games all the time." He raised his eyebrows, not waiting for an answer. "It's because he knows fencing isn't a *real* sport, that's why. It's something *sissies* do. Like dancing. Dad's *embarrassed* to have a son doing it."

For just a moment Kevin couldn't breathe. Dan was *right*. His father *was* embarrassed by him. How else to explain why he had taken so little interest in Kevin's fencing? This realization stabbed at Kevin as painfully as if his brother had driven a real sword through his gut.

"You know what, *Zitboy*," Kevin hissed furiously at Dan, trying to hurt him back by striking where he was most vulnerable. "You don't know *anything* about fencing. You don't know anything about *anything*. If you were ten times smarter than you are, you'd *still* be a moron."

And with that, Kevin Taylor stormed out of the room, as hurt as he had ever been.

CHAPTER 7

"Victory is reserved for those who are willing to
pay its price."

—Sun Tzu, *The Art of War*

The Present

John glared at the two weapons dealers with a hatred far beyond anything he had ever felt. He had no doubt they would carry
out their threat if he didn't cooperate. At that moment, his resistance broke entirely. A tear formed in the corner of his eye as
he glanced at the photos in his lap. The thought of the people he
loved being harmed by these savages—because of him—was more
than he could bear.

"Okay," he rasped softly, his tone one of complete surrender.
"I'll tell you what I know." He sighed and shook his head. "It
won't do you any good, anyway."

"For your family's sake," said Klaus, "you'd better hope you're
wrong about that."

Diego waited a moment for John to digest what his partner had
said and then began the interrogation. "So are the rumors true?"
he said calmly. "Was such a technology invented?"

John nodded.

"Who is the scientist running the project?" asked Klaus.

"A doctor of physics named Gateway. Stuart Gateway."

"And is this Dr. Gateway also the one who made the latest breakthrough in laser technology?" said the German

"That's right."

"Has this weapon—this Devil's Sword—been tested?" asked Diego.

"No. The president and the Joint Chiefs of Staff decided not to implement the new technology."

The mouths of both arms dealers dropped open in disbelief. "Impossible!" barked Klaus, his voice startling several nocturnal creatures that had just begun to venture out of their burrows and dens in the thick woods surrounding the clearing. "No government or military could *possibly* turn their back on the most powerful weapon the world has ever seen. You Americans are soft, but you're not *that* soft."

While his partner spoke, Diego was deep in thought. He stared into John's blue-green eyes knowingly. "But softness had nothing to do with this particular decision, did it my friend? The decision was made out of fear, not out of weakness. Wasn't it?"

John nodded wearily but said nothing.

"Fear of what?" Klaus demanded of the captive, still not understanding.

"Fear that if this weapon were deployed, an enemy might get their hands on it someday," replied John simply.

Diego nodded. "And their government is right to be afraid," he explained to his partner. "Whoever controlled such a weapon would shift the balance of world power away from the Americans. In fact, whoever controlled it would instantly become the dominant power on Earth. Since America is the dominant power already, why take any chances."

"This was their thinking," confirmed John. "In addition, Dr. Gateway threatened to resign if his discovery was ever used as a weapon. He had only signed on to the project because he had been promised what he built would be used for defensive purposes only."

"That figures," said Klaus scornfully. "American scientists are the softest of them all."

"The government ordered Gateway to destroy his notes and never duplicate his work," continued John, his voice raspy. The pain from his shattered arm was almost overwhelming, but he gritted his teeth and fought to ignore it. "He was happy to comply."

"Had he ever disclosed the scientific details of his breakthrough to anyone else?" asked Diego.

"No. So the discovery is now buried forever," said John. "That's it. A breakthrough in laser technology was made. Then it was purposely forgotten. End of story."

"So that's all there is to tell?" said Diego.

"That's all," said John emphatically.

Diego glared at him in disgust. "You're lying," he growled. "The rumors I heard say otherwise. So if this truly is the end of the story, your sisters and their families are about to have a very, very bad week," he threatened. "So no more games. If I even suspect you're lying from here on out, I'll have no mercy on any of them. Including little Joshua," he added with a scowl.

Hearing the name of his three-year-old nephew coming from the lips of a psychopath chilled John to the core.

"Now why don't you try again," said Diego evenly. "And this time I want the truth."

John Anderson nodded numbly. These men were ruthless and knew too much for him to risk attempting any further deceptions. Besides, it didn't matter. Nothing he told them would do them any good anyway. "Gateway built a working model, incorporating his breakthrough," he said.

"I assumed as much," said Diego. "After all, he had to test his theories. How else would he know it worked."

"The modifications to the laser were all internal. On the outside, the more powerful version looked exactly like the one scheduled to be launched on the satellite. The president ordered the more powerful version destroyed. The government and military are convinced that it was."

Diego thought about this for a moment, absently crushing an acorn under his foot as he did so. "I assume this means that it really wasn't," he said.

John hesitated for a moment and then sighed. "That's right," he said miserably. "Unknown to the politicians, my Black Ops unit defied the government. We made a switch. We installed the *new* laser on the satellite and destroyed the old. Only a handful of people know about this."

"But didn't the military realize the laser was far more powerful than expected the first time it was tested?" said Klaus.

John shook his head. "No. We never activated the modifications. Instead, we created a software program with all the proper passwords imbedded. Only if this software is transmitted to the satellite can the modifications be activated."

"Why go to so much trouble?" said Klaus. "Why not just activate it right away?"

"We didn't want to risk this weapon falling into enemy hands either. We only wanted to be able to boost the power in case of a dire emergency."

Klaus nodded. "I see," he said thoughtfully. "So even if an enemy did the impossible—took control of the satellite—they still couldn't use it as a weapon. First they would have to accomplish a *second* impossible task— stealing the software."

"*Exactly*. And that's why none of what I'm telling you will matter. You will *never* get your hands on this weapon!" said John. Despite being racked with pain and weak from loss of blood, his voice had momentarily become strong and filled with conviction.

"I wouldn't be so sure of that," said Diego.

John shook his head in contempt. "But I *am* sure. I've never been so sure of anything in my life," he spat. "Your actions today have gained you *nothing*. You have *no* idea what you're up against," he taunted. "The satellite control center and the software are in different locations, each exceedingly well protected. The satellite command codes are changed the moment anyone suspects anything is out of the ordinary. Gateway is the only civilian who knows the codes, and he's stationed at the most secure military base in the country," he finished defiantly.

Diego thought about this for a moment. "Nellis?" he guessed.

John didn't respond, but Diego could tell from the look in his eyes that he had guessed correctly.

Nellis Air Force Base was just outside of Las Vegas and encompassed a mysterious military installation known as Area 51. The nature of the work being done at this site was one of the most heavily guarded secrets in the country. Perhaps this secluded stretch of Nevada desert was used only to develop and test America's most advanced aircraft and weapons, but many believed that aliens or alien technology were kept here as well.

"Is the satellite control center at Nellis also?" asked Diego, even though he already knew the answer. After all, where else would it be?

John nodded unhappily.

"Tell me how Gateway is protected," demanded Diego.

John hesitated.

"Don't make me ask again!" warned the Cuban angrily.

"He has bodyguards assigned to protect him and his family while he's on the base," said John reluctantly. "And he almost never leaves. When he does, it's even worse. There is no advanced warning, and an *army* of bodyguards goes with him."

"What about this software?" continued Diego. "Where is it kept and how is it protected?"

"I don't know," said John. "Only the director of my agency does. I just know that it's extremely well protected and not at Nellis."

Diego eyed him skeptically.

John felt panic rise within him. If Diego thought he was lying his family would pay with their lives. "The director felt the fewer people who knew, the more secure it would be," he explained. "So I don't know anything more about it. That's the *truth,*" he continued adamantly. "*I swear it.*"

Diego stared deeply into John's blue-green eyes for several long seconds, as if taking the measure of his soul. "I believe you," he said finally. With that, he pointed his rifle at the Black Ops agent and pulled the trigger. The sound of the explosion reverberated throughout the darkening woods.

"Thanks for the help, Johnny," he said to what was now a lifeless body collapsed at the foot of the massive oak tree. "But we'll take it from here."

Klaus pulled a heavy, rubberized flashlight from his pocket and pointed it in the direction of the two helicopters at the other end of the clearing. Nightfall was almost complete and the beam cut through the darkness like a scalpel.

The two arms dealers began walking to their helicopter, not once looking back. They felt no need to bury the body or even hide it. Let the bacteria and the insects and the animals of the forest take it in due course. Even if it was discovered it wouldn't matter. The authorities had been after them for years. Adding another murder to their list of crimes wouldn't change a thing.

"That was useful information," said Klaus. "But he was right. This weapon is impossible to steal."

"And yet we're going to steal it anyway," said Diego smoothly.

"You're insane," said Klaus.

Diego laughed heartily. "Yes, my friend. But thought you already knew that."

"More insane than usual, I mean."

"How so?"

"It's a suicide mission."

"We acquire and sell arms, my friend," said Diego. "We're the best in the world at doing so. How can we not go after the most powerful weapon ever created? As the Americans say, this will be our Super Bowl."

Klaus shook his head adamantly.

"Consider this, then," said Diego. "Missile technology was our most profitable business. Not anymore. Not with this Heaven's Shield. On the other hand, any guesses as to what the Chinese, North Koreans, or Iranians would pay if we could deliver this Devil's Sword into their hands?"

This gave the German pause. "Billions and billions of dollars," he whispered. "We could name our price."

"So humor your loyal partner, won't you. For a project of this magnitude, anything we had to do to achieve our goal would be well worth it. Anything. Whatever we had to spend and whomever we had to kill along the way would be justified. If we had to hire an entire army of mercenaries, it would be a small price to pay."

Mercenaries were trained soldiers from around the world who went into business for themselves; selling their services to the highest bidder.

"With this freedom of action," continued Diego, "we can *do* this. No one can match our strategic thinking abilities. Are you telling me you aren't willing to give this any thought? With stakes this high?"

Klaus sighed heavily. "You're right. We should at least study it further. But if we haven't come up with a plan I fully support after a few weeks, than I'm done with the project. I'd rather be a living millionaire than a dead billionaire."

Diego chuckled. "Agreed," he said immediately.

They reached their small helicopter and Diego took the pilot's seat. "I propose that you recruit a few mercenaries to help out. Starting with a few who have already studied Nellis security. We need to find a weakness there we can exploit. I suspect we'll need far more manpower even than this, but let's start small and build our forces out as our needs become clearer."

"All right," said Klaus. "I'll get right on it. Naturally, we can never tell the hired help our real objective."

"Naturally," echoed Diego.

"What will *you* be doing?"

"I'll be spreading some money around to our collection of spies and computer hackers," said Diego. "Gathering more intelligence on the laser system. I'll also learn as much as I can about Dr. Gateway and his team."

Klaus nodded approvingly. "Sounds like a good start."

CHAPTER 8

"Wise men talk because they have something to
say; fools, because they have to say something."
—Plato, Ancient Greek Philosopher

Fifteen Months Earlier

Kevin usually didn't let his brothers get to him, but what Dan
had said had hurt him deeply and continued to hurt him every day.
His father was embarrassed that he was a fencer!

It wasn't fair! He had finally become passionate about a sport,
just like his father had always wanted. Now that he had, his father
was supposed to stop being disappointed in him. But that hadn't
happened. Instead, he was more disappointed in him than ever.

Kevin had thought everything was finally coming together in
his life. His father had been right: finding a sport he loved really
had been great for him. Lately he was as happy as he'd ever been.
But that had now changed. He still loved fencing, but it ate at him
that his father didn't approve of it and thought it was a sissy sport.

A sissy sport! Kevin didn't care what his brothers thought, but
how could his father not know better than this?

Kevin grew more sullen by the week. Now, on the rare occasions his father asked him about fencing he refused to talk about
it at all. His schoolwork began to suffer.

Three months after his spat with Dan, Kevin was on the phone with a kid named Ben, who was also a fencer and had become a friend. Their conversation soon turned to a girl named Rachel Felder with whom the boys fenced. At thirteen she was a year older than they were. Rachel was better than both of them, and Kevin spent a few minutes discussing possible ways to beat her.

A few minutes after Kevin ended the call he entered the family room. His brothers were sprawled like human speed bumps on two black-leather couches, watching TV. Cam was wearing high school issued gym shorts and a t-shirt, both green, while Dan was wearing a gray soccer outfit. Both looked as if they hadn't showered in a week. Dan shook his head sadly at Kevin as he approached. "Did I just hear what I thought I heard?"

"What are you talking about?"

"I overheard your conversation with your new geek friend," said Dan.

"His name is Ben," snapped Kevin. "So what were you doing, spying on me?" he added accusingly.

"Yeah, I was. See, you're like a science project, and I'm like that woman who lived among gorillas all those years. Except I'm not studying gorillas. I'm studying the social habits of the North American Super-Geek."

Cameron laughed.

Kevin's eyes narrowed angrily. "I'm sorry, but I didn't really catch that," he shot back at Dan. "As everyone knows, the idiotic babbling of the California Monkey-faced Jackass is hard to make out."

"Good comeback, Kev," said Cameron with a grin.

"Oh yeah, really good," said Dan sarcastically. "You really got me that time, Kevin," he added, rolling his brown eyes. "Well if you're having trouble hearing me, then listen closely, because this is important. I need you to tell me that I heard wrong. Please tell me that you aren't really fencing against a *girl!*"

Kevin furrowed his brow as the TV blared on in the background. "So?" he said. "What's the big deal?"

"What's the big deal!" repeated Dan, shifting from lying on his side to a seated position on the coach. "The big deal is that I told you fencing wasn't a real sport. I *told* you it was for sissies. But it's worse than I thought," he continued, shaking his head in disgust. "Not only are you fencing a girl, *you're losing to her.*"

"Shut up, moron. She's been doing it for three years and she's really good. So what!"

"She must be a Sith Lord to beat our Yoda," said Cam snidely, deciding to join in.

"I told you to take up a real sport," added Dan with a smirk. "Like ballet."

Kevin was about to reply when he noticed his father out of the corner of his eye standing on the staircase. He must have gotten home early from work and had been in his home office upstairs. He had heard the entire exchange *and he didn't look happy.* In fact, his eyebrows were drawn together fiercely and his nostrils flared like a bull about to charge

And this is exactly what he did; charging down the stairs to join his three sons in the family room. He turned off the TV as he passed it—doing this by hand instead of using the remote, which was *unheard* of—instantly signaling to his sons that he expected their full and total attention.

"Daniel, did you just say that fencing is for sissies?" he hissed icily. "That it's not really a sport?" He shook his head in disgust. "That's one of the dumbest things I've ever heard come out of your mouth."

Dan didn't respond. He just continued to face his father and blink nervously.

"Fencing is a *fantastic* sport," continued Mr. Taylor. "I had a friend who fenced in college and I went to some of his meets. It was amazing to watch. Good fencers are smart, athletic and blindingly fast. The competition is fierce and it's an exhaustive workout." He shook his head. "And it's *hardly* for sissies. If you get hit in the wrong place—even with the protective clothing—those swords can sting."

Kevin's mouth hung open. He shook his head as if he hadn't heard right. "You had a friend who fenced?" he said to his father, astonished. "You've been to matches? Why didn't you ever tell me that!" he demanded. "Dan said you never came to watch me because you didn't think fencing was a real sport. That you were *embarrassed* I was doing it."

If Mr. Taylor was angry before, his face was now a mask of fury the likes of which the boys had seen only a few times in their lives. The room was deathly silent, all three boys afraid to move or even breathe.

"*Daniel*," whispered their father chillingly. "*Is this true? Is this what you said?*"

Dan gulped. "Well I . . ." he began, stammering. "I . . . well, it's hard to remember," he said lamely. "Ah . . . it's possible that I said that," he finished.

Mr. Taylor could tell by the guilty look on Cameron's face that he had been part of this as well. "Daniel, Cameron," he barked. "Get in your rooms! *Now!*"

The boys didn't need to be told twice. Not when their dad was *this* steaming mad. As they bolted from the couches they were on and hustled up the stairs Mr. Taylor called after them. "The three of us are going to be having a long conversation when I'm done with Kevin," he said.

When Mr. Taylor heard two bedroom doors close upstairs, he turned to his youngest son. Kevin had no idea what to expect, but was relived to notice his father no longer looked angry. Instead, he looked apologetic and deeply concerned. He locked his gaze onto his youngest son's green eyes. "What Dan said couldn't be further from the truth, Kevin," he said softly. "It's true that I haven't come to watch you fence. But not because I was embarrassed. God no. I couldn't be prouder of you. You've been working hard and your coach tells me you're doing great."

The surprises just kept coming. "You've talked to Coach Bryant about me?"

His father nodded.

Kevin digested this for a moment. "So if you wanted to come watch me fence so badly," he said pointedly, "why didn't you?"

His father sighed. "I honestly didn't think you wanted me to. Ever since you were little you *hated* it when people watched you—especially when it came to sports."

Kevin frowned. He had to admit this was true.

"And I thought that maybe I pushed you too hard to like sports in the past, and that this was one of the reasons you never took to any of them. So this time I decided to back off completely. Leave you alone. So you wouldn't feel like I was putting any pressure on you. I've been holding my breath, trying not to screw this up, and hoping you would stick with it."

"Not liking those other sports had nothing to do with you putting pressure on me, Dad," said Kevin. "Although that *was* annoying," he added, rolling his eyes. "I just didn't like them enough to continue. It had nothing to do with you." He paused. "Fencing's different. I'm definitely going to keep fencing."

"Fantastic," said his father happily. "You know how strongly I believe that participation in a sport like this will do wonders for you. But just out of curiosity," he added, tilting his head. "*Why* is fencing different? What is it about it that you like so much?"

"That's easy, Dad," said Kevin with a grin. "I just really love stabbing people."

His father laughed. "Which comes in handy if you want to become either a great fencer or a great mass-murderer. I'm just relieved you chose fencing."

Kevin laughed as well. "But seriously," he said, "I like it because it's really challenging. You have to be fast, but that's not enough. You have to fake the other guy out. You need to use strategy."

"My roommate in college used to say good fencers needed to think two or three moves ahead. That it was like playing chess at a hundred miles an hour."

Kevin brightened. "Exactly," he said. "Just like in chess—or in war, for that matter—you have to play offense and defense at the same time. It's what baseball would be like if the ball was trying to hit *you* at the same time you were trying to hit *it*."

His father smiled. "I can see where this would make things more challenging," he said. "It's great to see you so enthusiastic about something. I'm really happy for you Kev. And as long as you're okay with it, I'd really love to come watch you."

Kevin smiled. "That would be great, Dad," he said without hesitation.

"Fantastic! I can't wait. You know, I was afraid to watch you or show a strong interest in case that put you off. But your mother's watched you a few times and reported good things back to me. And your coach raves about you."

"Really?"

"Really. He says you work hard, learn fast and are very coachable. And he says you have the one key thing that no coach can teach."

Kevin raised his eyebrows. "What's that?"

"Speed. Coach Bryant says you have the fastest hands he's seen in years."

Kevin beamed happily. The coach had never told him this.

"Well," said his father. "I had better go talk with your brothers."

"You aren't going to punish them, are you?" said Kevin worriedly, knowing that the harder their father was on them, the harder they would be on him when their parents weren't around.

"Don't worry, Kevin," said his father, as if reading his mind. "I'm just going to have a little discussion about knowing the difference between good-natured teasing and cruelty." He raised his eyebrows. "And perhaps it's time they learned a few things about the sport of fencing as well."

CHAPTER 9

"Accept the challenges so that you can feel the exhilaration of victory."

—General George S. Patton,
Fenced in the 1916 Olympics
Army's Youngest Ever 'Master of the Sword'
Designer of the Patton Saber

Mr. Taylor and his three sons arrived at the Excalibur Fencing Club for their scheduled appointment and entered. It was off-hours, so the club was empty. The room was about the size and shape of a basketball court. The plaster walls were painted red, and eight silver fencing strips were spaced evenly across it.

The coach heard them come in and greeted them warmly. He was just slightly under six feet in height, well muscled and extremely fit. He had a head of wavy, jet-black hair and a matching, neatly trimmed mustache that he had a habit of rubbing when he was deep in thought. His pale blue eyes stood out in sharp contrast to his black hair.

After coaching on the East Coast for many years he had come to San Diego just a few years earlier to open a studio of his own. Along with fencing he was accomplished in several styles of karate as well. Like Kevin's friend Ben the coach didn't say much—but when he did it was worth listening to.

Coach Bryant held up a thin steel sword, about a yard in length, with no sharp point or edges. It had a molded steel pistol grip, painted yellow, and a round silver dome, called a *bell guard,* just beyond the grip to protect a fencer's gloved hand and wrist. "This weapon is called a foil. It's the weapon your brother uses."

He handed the foil to Cam to examine.

As much as Cameron wanted to act bored, he couldn't help but be interested. There was a strange attraction to holding a sword, even if it was only a fencing weapon and not a real one. He gripped the handle and whipped it through the air several times in a crisscross pattern before handing it to Dan to inspect. Dan held the sword, moved several yards away, and sliced through the air as quickly as he could, not stopping until he attained the blade speed required for the foil to emit distinctive whooshing sounds.

"Well?" said Mr. Taylor to his older sons. "Are you two ready to suit up and try it?"

Dan blinked rapidly. "What?"

"I thought it would be fun for you and Cam to fence against Kevin here," he said. "The coach says he has plenty of equipment you can use."

"I thought you brought us here to get a history lesson or something," said Dan.

"Nope. I wanted to give you guys a chance to show off a little."

"Against *Kevin?*" said Cameron in disbelief. "I mean, I don't mind beating up on him, but it's not exactly a fair fight. He's twelve. I'm sixteen. Not to mention twice as tall and three times stronger." Cameron was already six feet in height and his muscles bulged from lifting weights for football.

The coach smiled. "Well, you're not quite *twice* as tall," he said. "But you do have a point. You have a huge height and strength advantage. You'll be able to lunge much farther than Kevin. And your father tells me you're very fast."

"A lot faster than Kevin, at least," he said. "I mean, again, he's only twelve."

"Kevin, are you willing to fight your brothers?" said Mr. Taylor.

A worried look crossed Kevin's face. "I guess so," he said, obviously not thrilled by the prospect.

"Good," said his father. "Then it's settled. Since you're the oldest, Cam, let's save you for last." He turned to his middle son. "Dan, are you ready to go?"

Dan smiled. He wasn't as tall or fast as Cameron yet, but he was still a lot taller and faster than his little brother. "Bring it on," he said arrogantly.

Kevin was already wearing his fencing gear. To save time, Dan and Cameron suited up together. Each put on long white pants and a white fencing jacket. Not counting the thick glove they would wear, the last piece of clothing they both donned was called a lamé— pronounced *lah-may*, in the same way café was pronounced ka-fay. This was a woven-steel vest, typically silver-gray in color, put on over the jacket. The lamé vest covered every inch of the target area. At many clubs fencers routinely had their last names stenciled on the back of these vests, and many added the word *USA* below their names as well.

Once Cam and Dan were suited up, Coach Bryant showed them the proper stance, how to lunge, various ways to block their opponent's blade—which was called parrying—and the proper way to retreat. After ten minutes they were eager to start.

"Since the tip of the blade can move faster than the eye can follow," explained the coach, "we'll be using electric scoring."

Kevin was already hooked up at one end of the strip and waiting patiently. The coach pulled a long, spaghetti-thin cord from a retractable reel at Dan's end of the strip. After a few manipulations, it was attached to his sword and clipped to the back of his waist like a leash. He looked like a diver hooked up to an oxygen line. As Dan moved forward he would pull additional cord from the reel. As he retreated the cord would retract back into the reel.

Coach Bryant instructed the two boys to meet in the middle of the strip. "Stab your brother gently in the chest," he told Dan. The tip of the foil was a tiny, spring-loaded metal button that would compress upon contact with a solid object. Dan pushed the tip of the foil into Kevin's metallic lamé and a red light appeared on the electronic scoring display attached to the wall.

"To score you have to compress the tip with a force of 500 grams," the coach explained to Dan. "Duels used to be fought until first blood. So this is the same force it would take to break the skin and draw blood if you were using a real sword."

The coach paused. "Foil fencing has the smallest target area of any of the fencing styles. In foil fencing you can only score with the tip of the sword, and only a strike to the torso counts. You don't get points for hitting the arms or head or lower body."

"How many other styles of fencing are there?" asked Cameron.

"Three altogether. Foil, epee and saber. Each one uses a different type of weapon. An Epee sword is stiffer and heavier than a foil sword. In Epee fencing you can score by hitting anywhere on the body, including the feet." The coach paused. "The saber has long been the weapon of Cavalries around the world."

"And Jedi Knights, of course," said Dan, smirking.

The coach ignored him. "In saber fencing," he continued, "strikes count anywhere above the waist, including the head and arms. And you can score points by hitting your opponent with the *edge* of the blade also, instead of just the tip." The coach raised his eyebrows. "Makes sense, doesn't it? When you're on top of a horse, it's a lot easier to slash down at your enemies with your sword than to hit them with the point."

Cameron thought about the scores of movies he had seen over the years in which horsemen had hacked through armies of foot soldiers, and he had to admit that in every one of them there had been plenty of downward slashing by those on horseback.

"But let me get back to the duel at hand," said Coach Bryant. "In foil fencing, the lamé vests cover the entire target area. So Daniel, when you compress the tip anywhere on Kevin's lamé, front or back, you'll trigger a red light on the scoring display. If Kevin hits *you* on target, a green light goes on, indicating that it's his touch, or point."

"Got it," said Dan.

"Good. There will be three, three-minute periods, with one-minute breaks in between. First one to fifteen touches wins—or whoever is in the lead if time runs out."

"What if we hit each other at the same time?" asked Dan.

"Good question. When both lights come on at once, the ref has to decide who had what is called 'right of way', and this fencer is awarded the touch. It can get a little tricky. Basically, the fencer who begins his attack first has right of way. But if he stops his attack, misses, or his attack is deflected by the defender, the other guy has right of way—as long as he attacks back immediately. If not, the first fencer to attack again has the right of way."

"*What?*" said Dan in frustration, looking at the coach as if he had been speaking Greek.

"Don't worry," said the coach with a grin. "This is your first bout, so if both lights come on, I'll give *you* the point."

"Doesn't that make this even less fair to Kevin?" asked Cam.

"You two aren't familiar with the rules," the coach replied. "That's not fair either. Besides," he added with a hint of a smile. "Whoever said life was fair?"

After a few words of instruction for Dan on how to do so, both fencers saluted each other and the coach, who was reffing the bout, with their swords. This was a tradition and was repeated at the conclusion of the bout, at which time the fencers would also shake hands.

With the preliminaries completed, Dan held up his sword. "My name is Inigo Montoya," he announced in a Spanish accent, mimicking a famous scene from the movie, *The Princess Bride*. "You killed my father. Prepare to die."

It was clear Dan wasn't taking the bout very seriously.

When the coach called for them to fence, Dan came out like an enraged panther, lunging and stabbing at his brother with great speed, but Kevin calmly parried all of his attacks, maintaining a perfect distance from his brother. Suddenly, Kevin dropped to the ground, crouching low like a frog, and stabbed straight up, completely surprising his brother. A green light appeared on the scoring display.

"Attack arrives from my right. Touch for Kevin," announced the coach.

Dan shook his head in disgust. That was lucky. Kevin wouldn't surprise him like that again. He was annoyed with himself for letting the little runt get even a single point.

Dan snarled under his mask. *"My name is Inigo Montoya,"* he said again, far more forcefully than he had before. *"You killed my father. Prepare to die!"*

And this time, he sounded as if he really meant it.

CHAPTER 10

"It's not the size of the dog in the fight, it's the size of the fight in the dog."
　　　　　　　　—Mark Twain, American Author

The two boys came at each other again. This time, Kevin purposely rushed in so he was within a few inches of his brother. Dan tried to move his arm far enough back so he could hit Kevin with the tip of his sword, but Kevin was too close. Kevin, on the other hand, had shorter arms and calmly buried the tip of his sword in his brother's chest. A green light came on.

"Attack arrives, touch right. Kevin leads two touches to zero."

For the third touch, Kevin didn't resort to anything his brother might consider trickery. The boys scurried up and down the long strip for an extended period of time. Finally, Kevin attacked, and when his brother moved to parry the attack, he anticipated it, moving his blade around the parry so Dan didn't block his blade after all. He then lunged forward in a single, smooth motion and was rewarded with a green light.

Dan got the next point. As good as Kevin was, Dan was still a superb athlete, and he was finally able to use his blazing speed to hit his younger brother in the stomach.

"You're gonna be road kill now!" announced Dan triumphantly through his heavy black mask. "It just took me a few minutes to catch on."

Kevin shook his head. His brother was an *idiot*. The point really should have been awarded to Kevin since both lights had come on and it was Kevin's right of way, but the coach was being nice. "*I'm* gonna be road kill?" said Kevin with a laugh. "You still aren't getting it, are you, Newby," he continued. "You don't have a chance, but you're just too dumb to know it."

This comment further enraged Dan and he came after his little brother like a kid possessed, but when the first three-minute period ended Kevin was leading six touches to two.

As the boys took their one-minute break, Mr. Taylor approached Kevin on his end of the strip. He motioned for his son to remove his mask. "Flick him in the leg," he whispered in Kevin's ear. By flick, he meant wielding the sword like it was a whip.

"*What?*" Kevin whispered back in shock.

"That's part of the sport, right? I mean, it happens by accident all the time, doesn't it? I'll bet you've been hit off target like that dozens of times, and you bounced right back."

Kevin nodded. "Yeah, but Coach Bryant would kill me if he thought I did it on *purpose*."

"Good," whispered his father approvingly. "Normally, I would too. But this is a special case. It would happen naturally if Dan fenced for any length of time. But this will probably be the last time he fences in his entire life. So I just want to make sure he gets the full fencing experience."

Thirty seconds into the second period, Kevin carried out his father's request and flicked his blade into Dan's upper thigh.

"Ahhhh!" yelled Dan, dropping his sword arm and hopping around on one foot as if the leg had been splattered by lava. "*Holy sh...*" he bellowed, just able to bite off the second word in time. He rubbed his leg furiously, wincing in pain.

"Are you okay there, Danny?" his father asked innocently, barely managing to fight back laughter.

Dan was still wincing but fought to act as macho as he possibly could. "Absolutely," he croaked through tightly clenched teeth. "No problem."

"Good," said his father. "Because everyone here knows this is just a sissy activity. You know, like ballet. So I'd hate to think a tiny off-target hit like that would cause you any discomfort."

"None at all," lied Dan, still rubbing his leg.

Less than five minutes later the bout was over. Kevin had crushed his older brother fifteen to four.

Dan couldn't believe it! How had this happened? Not only was he furious, he realized he was sweaty and was gasping for breath. Racing up and down the silver strip for even a few minutes with the explosive speed necessary to avoid a fast moving sword being thrust at your gut was exhausting. Especially when doing so in a fencing stance.

Dan was fuming. He had been totally humiliated by the little runt.

But only seven minutes later his anger turned into a reluctant respect. And for very good reason. His little brother did the same thing to Cam! In fact, Kevin beat Cam worse than he had beaten Dan. Fifteen to three! Cameron was bigger and faster even than Dan was, but it almost seemed that this worked in Kevin's favor, providing a bigger target for his blade. Kevin had worked Cameron over effortlessly; a David who seemed always able to dance just out of reach of Goliath's sword.

"Incredible," said Cam as he pulled off his mask, sweat dripping from his face. He and Kevin saluted each other and the coach with their swords and then shook hands. "How did you do that, Kevin?" he said in frustration, but with a touch of actual admiration.

Kevin beamed happily. Part of him wanted to gloat and rub it in. But he didn't. He was too busy relishing the fact that for the first time in his life his brothers were actually showing respect for his abilities in a sport.

But nothing was going to stop their father from rubbing it in further. "Good thing I didn't have you guys face Kevin's thirteen-year-old friend, Rachel. Then you two would have been beaten even worse," he said with a grin. "By a girl! A girl as petite as they come." Their father laughed. "Now *that's* something I'd pay good money to see."

"You knew this would happen, didn't you Dad?" said Cam, realizing just how completely they had been set up.

"Let's just say I suspected you two would underestimate the importance of training and experience," he replied. "And your brother's skill."

"Your father's right," added Coach Bryant. "Your brother is very talented. And in fencing, speed and skill are more important than strength and height."

"Good work, Kevin," said Mr. Taylor, putting his arm around his youngest son and leading him out of the room. "I can't tell you how much I enjoyed that," he added, flashing a broad smile over his shoulder at Cameron and Dan, still shell-shocked from the beating they had taken from their younger brother.

Kevin was sure he was now glowing like a neon sign. Because as good as it felt to have earned the respect of his brothers, earning the respect of his father felt even better.

CHAPTER 11

"Friendships born on the field of athletic strife
are the real gold of competition."

—Jesse Owens, Four-Time Olympic
Gold Medalist (Track & Field)

The Present

Who could have believed it! Kevin Taylor hadn't even known
the sport of fencing existed until he was twelve. Now, just two
years later, he was in the finals of the San Diego fourteen-and-
under tournament. Even better, he was fencing against his close
friend, Ben, for the gold. His other good friend, Rachel Felder, was
in the crowd.

And both of his parents as well.

And more impossible still, Dan and Cameron. His older brothers had surprised him, appearing in the crowd for the finals as if
by magic, and actually rooting for him loudly.

The three brothers still teased and tormented each other fre-
quently, but ever since Dan and Cameron had fenced against him,
fifteen months earlier, Kevin's relationship with his older brothers
had changed. They never again suggested fencing wasn't really a
sport or was for sissies. Although they would never admit it, Kevin

knew they respected him for his fencing abilities. And they began to take an interest in his progress.

Kevin had continued to improve every month. By the time he turned thirteen he was beginning to win local youth tournaments and even medal in some adult events. He was getting a reputation among kids in the San Diego fencing community as the kid to beat. And as his successes in fencing grew, so too did his confidence— in all aspects of life. And while he would never be truly outgoing, he had lost much of his shyness.

Not only that, but he had grown a full four inches! While he was still short, he was inching his way toward average height. Even better, his braces had finally come off. He was happier than he had ever been.

"The rest period is over," announced the referee. "Fencers to the *en garde* line," he said, using the traditional French pronunciation of *on guard*.

Kevin pulled on his mask for the third and final period. Ben was good, but Kevin fenced him often and won most of the time. He was exhausted from the long day of fencing but confident he could hold on over the last three minutes of the bout.

Kevin's and Ben's swords clashed furiously as they raced over the silver strip, exploding forward and backward like tightly coiled springs, attacking or trying to hurl themselves beyond reach of the other's attacking blade. Despite Ben's heroic efforts, Kevin's lead only increased. When time ran out, Kevin led thirteen to seven. He had won!

Kevin was giddy as he shook hands with Ben, whose straight, coal-black hair was glistening with sweat. Although both of Ben's parents had come from China, he had been born in San Diego and had lived there his entire life.

"Good job, Kevin," said Ben earnestly. His loss to his friend didn't trouble him. He knew Kevin was the better fencer, and he was as happy as he could be to take home the silver medal.

"You too, Ben," said Kevin happily.

As soon as the handshake was completed, Kevin's family surrounded him on the strip, showering him with congratulations. His brothers, of course, couldn't bring themselves to compliment him outright, but rather had to disguise any compliment within the cloak of an insult.

"Not bad for a pathetic loser with no athletic ability," said Cameron, patting Kevin on the back warmly.

"Yeah," said Dan, now almost six feet tall himself. "You may be the most feeble kid on the planet, but I have to admit you aren't half bad with a sword in your hand."

Ben's parents congratulated their son as well, but in a far quieter and more reserved manner.

Mr. and Mrs. Taylor had driven separately and after the medal ceremony Cameron and Dan left with their mother. Mr. Taylor would be taking Kevin home.

Kevin and Ben chatted happily in the locker room about the tournament while they stripped off their lamés and now-pungent outer garments. Although their friend Rachel was only fifteen-years-old, and so short and petite that she still weighed under a hundred pounds, she had taken silver in the girls' sixteen-and-under event. The boys were eager to talk to her about the tournament as well when they were finished changing.

Rachel Felder was as smart as she was tough, and that was saying something. When she was three years old, her father had left her and her mother. He had disappeared one day, never to be heard from again. Her mother quickly began to feel sorry for herself and within a year had become an alcoholic. She bounced from long periods of sobriety to long periods of drunkenness, and from job to job to job. Rachel, an only child, was forced to grow up in a hurry, having to take care of her mother more often than her mother took care of her. As if this wasn't bad enough, her difficulties at home prevented her from ever really fitting in at school, and she was bullied unmercifully because of it.

Most kids would have become bitter at being forced to endure such a hard life. Rachel Felder was not most kids. Despite every hardship that was thrown at her, she remained optimistic and hopeful. She was determined not to feel sorry for herself or ever play the role of a victim.

Because of her determination she never backed down when she was bullied. Not once. And while this resulted in her getting beat up a lot in the early days, she quickly became so good at defending herself that the bullying ceased. Now she was liked and respected by almost everyone: known to be as loyal a friend as she was formidable an enemy.

She was naturally bright and worked hard at her studies, a combination that made her one of the top students in her school. But that didn't mean she was prim and proper. Just the opposite. She loved to laugh and found humor in almost everything. Despite all the difficulties she faced on a regular basis, she was relentlessly friendly and cheerful. Her easy, infectious smile brought a sparkle to her eyes that lit up her face.

Her life had changed dramatically almost five years earlier when her school had held an assembly and invited Coach Bryant to demonstrate the sport of fencing. She had become hooked immediately. As hard as she worked at her studies, she worked even harder to learn fencing. The coach thought the world of her and their relationship was very close. Of all of the students at *Excalibur,* only Rachel put in more hours than Kevin. She had been a mainstay at the club when Kevin first arrived, and when she realized he shared her passion for fencing she had generously shown him the ropes, and introduced him to the tight-knit community of San Diego fencers.

Kevin and Ben finished changing and exited the boys' locker room, each now wearing a medal dangling down from a colorful ribbon around their necks. Rachel soon joined them, wearing a medal of her own. Like the lustrous hair falling between her shoulder blades, her face still had a reddish hue from hours of tough physical exertion. "Not a bad showing for the kids from the *Excalibur Fencing Club,*" she noted cheerfully.

"What about the six other kids from *Excalibur* who all got knocked out in the early rounds?" asked Ben.

"So? It's not like all nine *Excalibur* kids entered in the tournament could win," she pointed out. "I mean, that would be pretty tough given that they don't award nine gold medals per event." She paused. "I'm pretty sure I read that once in the official rules of fencing," she said with a grin.

"You're right," conceded Ben. "Good point." Ben lifted the silver disk from his chest and raised his eyebrows. "But would it be too much to ask for them to award just *two* gold medals per event?" he said wryly. "That's all I'm saying."

Everyone laughed. Rachel held up her own silver metal. "Not such a bad idea at that," she said impishly.

CHAPTER 12

"There is no such thing as chance; and what seems to us merest accident springs from the deepest source of destiny."

—Friedrich von Schiller, German Philosopher

Ted Taylor congratulated Coach Bryant on the strong performances of his students and watched his son from the corner of his eye chatting and laughing with Ben and Rachel, medals around each of their necks. The close friendship and camaraderie between the three of them was plain to see, and Mr. Taylor couldn't have been happier for his son.

Coach Bryant glanced in the direction of the three fencers as well. "I really can't take credit for their success. They've earned it themselves. They work their tails off," he said, rubbing his dark mustache absently. "You should be very proud of Kevin," he said. After a few moments of silence he added, "Speaking of that, do you have a minute?"

"Sure," replied Ted Taylor.

The coach led him out of the fencing area and entered the storage room that doubled as his office. While the coach was always impeccably groomed and maintained a spotless personal appearance, his office was a total mess. Fencing weapons that needed repair were strewn about, often in pieces, together with foam swords he used to teach young children, fencing books, and assorted tools.

"Kevin has made remarkable progress," began Coach Bryant. "It's safe to say he's now the best fourteen-yearold foilist in San Diego. So I think it's time to challenge him further. I'd like him to compete in some regional tournaments. Face other kids who are the best in *their* cities."

"Are you sure he's ready for that?

The coach nodded. "I think he's more than ready. So are Ben and Rachel for that matter. I think Kevin may even be good enough to medal at the regional level, although that remains to be seen."

"Okay," said Ted Taylor, swelling with pride but trying not to let it show. "If you think he's ready, I'm in full support."

"Great. There's a regional tournament coming up in about six weeks that looks pretty good," he said, glancing at a page of information he had printed out from the Internet the night before. "That's a week after the kids get out of school for the summer. They're calling it 'The Desert Challenge'. It's in Las Vegas."

Mr. Taylor nodded. This was well within driving distance.

"You think Kevin might be interested?" said the coach.

"No doubt about it," said Mr. Taylor. "Where is it being held? A school?"

"Actually, it's being held at a military base there. Apparently the commander of the base is a big fencing nut."

"I didn't know there was a military installation in Las Vegas," said Mr. Taylor.

"Me neither," admitted the coach. He scanned the information sheet yet again. "It's at a place called Nellis Air Force Base."

Mr. Taylor shrugged. "Okay," he said. "Nellis Air Force Base it is." He couldn't wait to tell his son about the tournament. "I'm sure this will be an exciting experience for Kevin," he said.

"No doubt about it," agreed the coach. "A very exciting experience, indeed."

PART TWO

"All warfare is based on deception. Hence, when able to attack, we must seem unable; when using our forces, we must seem inactive; when we are near, we must make the enemy believe we are far away; when far away, we must make him believe we are near."

—Sun Tzu, *The Art of War*

CHAPTER 13

"Seize the moment. Man was never intended to
become an oyster."
—Theodore Roosevelt, US President
Took Fencing Lessons in the White House

Kevin couldn't wait for *The Desert Challenge* to finally arrive.
Not only was this his first regional tournament but the coach had
gotten permission for Ben and Rachel to compete as well. Their
parents had even agreed to let them all arrive a day early to watch
the adult events, and even better, to vacation in Vegas for a few
days afterwards.

What could be better!

Mr. Taylor had offered to accompany Coach Bryant and the
three outstanding young fencers from San Diego. Now that he
knew Kevin didn't mind being watched he had become his biggest
fan.

But if Kevin's excitement was great, Rachel's was even greater.
She had never been to Vegas. In fact, she had never been *anywhere*.
Her mother wasn't one for travel—in fact, was afraid of flying—
and Rachel had never been more than a few hundred miles away
from San Diego in her entire life.

Finally, it was time. Everyone met at *Excalibur* at the crack
of dawn on Saturday morning and piled into an oversized,

twelve-passenger minivan. The van was bright yellow and had an advertisement for the club on its side.

The five-hour drive went by surprisingly fast. They quickly checked into their motel, the *Lucky Days Motor Lodge,* located just a few miles from Nellis and away from the touristy and more expensive parts of Vegas. The motel was just a single line of rooms stretched along a poorly maintained parking lot. They had rented two adjoining rooms for the five of them.

Less than thirty minutes later they pulled up to the guard gate at Nellis Air Force Base. At long last, the fun and excitement they had been eagerly awaiting was finally becoming a reality.

Nellis security had required all visitors to supply copies of their photo IDs weeks before the tournament, and had made it clear that extensive background checks would be performed. An armed guard approached the car holding a German Shepherd by a short leash.

"We're here for the fencing tournament," said the coach.

The guard nodded, absently stroking the dog's back. He collected ID from the two adults and consulted a thick binder containing the names and photographs of all visitors that were expected that day. After about thirty seconds he returned the identification and asked the three teenagers their names, checking them in as well.

After asking permission, the guard had the German Shepherd sniff their luggage and fencing bags.

Rachel leaned in close to Kevin. "You didn't leave any dirty gym socks in there, did you?" she whispered softly into his ear. "Because the slightest whiff of *those* and that dog's a goner for sure," she finished, fighting back laughter.

Kevin grinned broadly as the dog finished its inspection. Finally, the guard handed the coach a map of Area 1 and traced out the route to the base gymnasium, the site of the tournament. "You are only authorized to drive between here and there, and you must remain inside the gym at all times while you're on the base."

And just like that, they were inside Nellis. While this didn't mean much to the others, Kevin was as excited as he could be. They were actually on a base that housed nuclear weapons, Area 51, and top-secret weapons research facilities. Incredible!

Before Kevin had discovered fencing he had spent endless hours playing computer war games. Not the typical shoot-'em-up style video games, but those that required complex strategies. In one such game, he commanded vast armies, forged alliances with other nations, and fought simulated battles across the globe, arming his soldiers with computer-simulated versions of actual, modern equipment. Whenever he resumed play in this game, quotes from generals, warlords, brilliant strategists, and famous thinkers throughout history would appear on his screen, delivering pearls of wisdom— military and otherwise. He found many of these quotes fascinating and even wrote down the ones he liked best in what he called, "The Notebook of Cool Quotes."

Even now, whenever he had a few hours to spare, he played an Internet game against other online players that required extensive knowledge of military equipment and major U.S. military installations. And no base was as important, or as mysterious, as Nellis. He couldn't believe his luck to actually be here.

Minutes later they entered the gymnasium that housed the tournament. It was gigantic, housing four full-size basketball courts with room to spare. The ceiling was thirty feet high and the vast, open room dwarfed the hundreds of people within it.

Fencers of every size, all dressed in white, were scattered in every direction. Dozens of temporary fencing strips had been laid down at even intervals over the glossy hardwood floor and the hustle and bustle of the tournament was electric. Everywhere they looked, bouts were in progress. The sounds of spectators rooting, refs shouting *halt*, and numerous pairs of swords clashing echoed against the distant ceiling and walls and arrived at their ears from all directions. A large stand selling food and drinks was set up in one corner of the gym, manned by volunteers.

They watched talented adult fencers for hours while Coach Bryant pointed out their strengths and weaknesses. In the middle of one such lesson the coach stopped and pointed to one of two armorer's tables that had been set up at either end of the building. Armorers were responsible for certifying that the equipment of all participants in a tournament was up to snuff. "You should check your equipment now," said Coach Bryant to his three students. "The line is the shortest I've seen it."

The three *Excalibur* fencers didn't need to be told twice. Armorer lines were painfully slow. They had never even been to a tournament that allowed the equipment check to be done the day before the event and this was their chance to get it over with.

Only three fencers were in line ahead of them when they arrived. They happily joined the short line. Moments later another kid about their age fell in behind them. He was several inches shorter even than Kevin, slight of build, and his brown hair was cut very short. A soldier in full uniform approached him. "I have to go now, Matt," he said. "But I'm planning to watch you fence for about an hour tomorrow before I go on duty."

"Great," said the kid pleasantly as the soldier headed for an exit. "See you then."

"Impressive," said Rachel in a friendly tone to the kid, apparently named Matt. "You haven't even checked in yet and you've already got Nellis soldiers on your side. How'd you manage that?"

Matt grinned. "Not so impressive, really. My secret is that I live here."

"Wow," said Ben. "It must be fun to live in Vegas."

Matt shook his head. "No. I mean I live *here*. At Nellis. I have since I can remember. So I know a lot of the guys."

"Cool," said Rachel. "How lucky are you, choosing fencing as a sport and then finding out there's an awesome tournament like this in your own back yard."

Matt laughed. "It's actually the other way around," he said. "I'm only a fencer *because* of the tournament. The top general at Nellis loves fencing, so five years ago he started hosting this tournament on base. They have it here every year. My father took me to watch the first year, when I was nine, because I was always running around hitting things with a toy light-saber. Anyway, once I saw real fencing I knew right away I had to do it. And I have been ever since. We have a club right here on base."

They all continued talking while they presented their equipment, one at a time, for testing. The armorer made sure there were no defects in their masks that would allow a sword to penetrate and there were no "dead spots" in their lamés that would fail to register a hit. The visitors from San Diego peppered Matt with questions about Nellis, joked around, and in general became quite friendly with him.

While they talked Kevin had the strange feeling that two men, who appeared to be watching a nearby bout, were actually watching the four of them out of the corner of their eyes.

Nah, he thought. He must be imaging things.

Matt seemed like a really good kid, and they learned he would be fencing in the same event as Ben and Kevin. Kevin told him he had only been fencing for two years and that this was his first event outside of San Diego. "My name is Kevin, by the way," he said. "Kevin Taylor. And this is Rachel Felder and Ben Chang," he added, pointing to each in turn. "I'm sure we'll be seeing a lot of each other tomorrow."

"No doubt about it," said Matt. "I'll be rooting for you to win the girl's sixteens, Rachel," he said earnestly. He grinned at Kevin and Ben. "As for you two, I can only root for you to come in second and third."

Ben laughed. "I'll take either one of those," he said. "Good luck to you also. Your name is Matt, right?"

The boy nodded. "That's right," he said affably. "Matt Gateway."

CHAPTER 14

"Courage is not the lack of fear. It is acting in spite of it."

—Mark Twain

Kevin yawned, despite the loud music booming from a portable speaker connected to his I-pod. It had been a long day. They had awoken at the crack of dawn and they had accomplished a lot, including a 300mile drive. Even Rachel looked a little tired and she had more energy than anyone Kevin had ever known.

The three kids hung out in one room while the adults were in the other, but this was only a temporary arrangement. The adults were currently in Rachel's room. When it was time for bed she would get this room to herself while the four males would share the other one. The boys had complained about this arrangement, but the coach had reminded them that swordfighters were nothing if not chivalrous. Rachel needed her privacy.

Kevin was seated on the front end of a cot, a few feet away from two thin, wooden doors that closed off the passageway between the two adjoining rooms. Both had been temporarily locked shut since they tended to stay slightly ajar otherwise, and the two adults weren't big fans of the kids' music.

Kevin pulled his fencing bag next to him and removed one of the two foils he had brought—the minimum requirement. Most of the fencers at this tournament would bring many more weapons than this. Fencers were required to wrap the last six or seven inches of their foils with insulating tape—leaving the tip free of tape so it could compress properly, of course—to help ensure hits were registered correctly. The night before a tournament, Kevin routinely re-taped his blades and adjusted his grips if necessary.

Coach Bryant and Kevin's father were in the other room watching the news. There was a knock on their outside door. Mr. Taylor raised his eyebrows. For a moment he thought it might be a motel neighbor complaining about the music, but the room the kids were in was the last one at one end of the motel, so they were the only ones who could hear it.

"Are you expecting anyone?" he asked the coach.

Coach Bryant shook his head as Ted Taylor walked the short distance to the door and peered through the peephole.

An elderly man stood patiently at the door, slightly stooped over, his face wrinkled and his hair gray. Mr. Taylor opened the door a few inches to find out what he wanted, leaving the chain attached. "Can I help you?" he said.

"Is that your yellow van parked around the corner?" asked the man. His speech was slow and tired and his voice raspy.

"It is," said Mr. Taylor, wondering where this was going.

"Good," said the man, nodding more slowly than Mr. Taylor had thought was possible. "Glad I found you. Your lights are on. Woulda turned 'em off myself but your van's locked."

"Thanks," said Mr. Taylor appreciatively.

"Don't mention it, son," rasped the man as Mr. Taylor gently closed the door.

The coach had heard the entire exchange. "I'll take care of it," he said. He fished the car keys from his pocket and headed for the door as Mr. Taylor returned to the edge of the bed to continue watching the news.

The coach undid the chain on the door and pushed it halfway open when the totally unexpected happened.

The door pushed back!

Hard.

Someone had been lying in wait behind it!

Caught off guard, the coach was thrown backwards by the force of the door while three commandoes stormed into the room, all dressed in black. The first one through held what looked like a .45 semiautomatic pistol in front of him and squeezed off a shot while the coach was still stumbling backwards.

Ted Taylor's heart stopped as he looked on helplessly, expecting blood to erupt from the coach as the large caliber slug tore through his body. But there was no blood. Had the shot missed? Impossible.

And then Mr. Taylor realized the gun hadn't been a .45 after all. Instead of bullets, it had fired a small tranquilizer dart that was now imbedded in Coach Bryant's neck. The coach pulled out the dart but its payload had already taken effect. He slumped to his knees and then slid to the ground, unconscious.

Mr. Taylor reacted instantly, reaching for a lamp from the table in front of him to use as a weapon. But the second commando through the door didn't hesitate, burying a tranquilizer dart in his chest before he could lift the lamp. Ted Taylor fell unconscious seconds later as the fast-acting tranquilizer surged through his bloodstream.

A fourth commando burst through the open door, followed closely by the elderly man who had lured the coach outside.

Only he wasn't as elderly as he had appeared.

In fact, he now walked briskly, with athletic grace, and the bearing of his face had changed dramatically. His wig and makeup were still in place. But his quick eyes, darting around to take in the scene, and equally quick movements were those of a well-trained soldier in the prime of his life. He knelt down and removed the car keys from the coach's outstretched hand as he lay sprawled on the room's worn, gray carpeting. "I'll pull up their fencing van," he said softly to the group of commandoes. "You four load these men inside."

One of the black-clad men pointed at the door to the adjoining room. "What about the kids, Diego?" he asked quietly.

"We'll take care of them in a minute," whispered the Cuban. They had taken out the two men without making much noise, and judging from the laughter and loud music coming through the adjoining doors the kids hadn't heard a thing. "First things first."

Diego backed up the yellow van to within ten feet of the door and watched to be sure no one could see his men loading the two prisoners inside. It was a dark night and the motel was poorly lighted, so even if someone was watching they wouldn't be able to tell for sure what was going on.

Once the two unconscious men were inside the vehicle, Diego jumped from the driver's seat onto the pavement and motioned to two of his men. "Wolf and Dimitri," he said, "you're with me. The rest of you take this van back to the house. We'll round up the kids and meet you there." He handed the keys to a Korean mercenary named Ahn. "Go!" he ordered.

Within seconds the fencing van with its human cargo had pulled onto the road and began steadily gaining speed.

Diego removed his own keys from his front pocket and faced Wolf and Dimitri. "I'll get the SUV ready," he said. "You two gather up the kids." He paused until he was sure he had the complete attention of the two soldiers. "Remember, I need them in perfect condition. If they're injured in any way, heads will roll." He stared at them icily. "*Your* heads. Is this understood?"

"Don't worry, Diego," said the mercenary called Dimitri, who was completely bald and had dark tattoos covering most of his body. "We'll be gentle." He smiled cruelly. "After all, there's a first time for everything."

The two men returned to the room they had just invaded and quietly unlocked the adjoining door on their side. Wolf—a Pakistani mercenary so named because his hairy, elongated face showed a remarkable likeness to this dangerous predator—pushed gently on the adjoining door on the kids' side. It didn't budge. The small deadbolt lock must have been engaged, which was unexpected. He readied his gun and rapped three times on the door in quick succession with his left hand.

Upon hearing this, Kevin shot a quick glance at his watch before returning his attention once again to re-taping his foils. It was 9:45. The coach had wanted everyone to switch rooms at ten so they could get plenty of sleep for the big day ahead. This must be the fifteen-minute warning.

"We *know*," he said loudly at the door. "We'll send the, um . . . damsel over in fifteen minutes." He glanced at Rachel and grinned as he said this, and she rolled her eyes. Few girls were less the pampered, helpless damsel type than she was.

After a brief pause there was another rap at the door.

Were the adults going deaf? Kevin thought irritably. "We *got* it," he said, louder this time, continuing to wind a piece of black tape around the top portion of his blade. "I'm in the middle of something. Let Rachel listen to a few last songs and we'll kick her out, okay."

On the other side of the door Wolf glanced meaningfully at Dimitri. If they spoke they would give themselves away, and shooting at the lock or kicking down the door would risk injury to one or more of the kids. Wolf was getting impatient and rapped on the door once again, more urgently this time.

Kevin shook his head in exasperation. Maybe this wasn't the fifteen-minute warning after all. But had the coach and his father suddenly lost their ability to speak? *"Tell us what you want already!"* bellowed Kevin.

There was no answer. Kevin glanced at his friends questioningly. Ben just shrugged. Rachel spread her hands helplessly and said, "Maybe this is a weird practical joke. Let's find out what's going on."

Although Kevin was closest to the adjoining door, he was holding a foil and had a roll of tape in his lap. Rachel hopped off the edge of the bed she was sitting on and retracted the tiny dead-bolt from the door, swinging it open.

Wolf shot through the opening! Keeping his body against the door so it couldn't be re-shut, he pointed his gun at Ben, who was sitting on his bed preparing to kick off his shoes. "Move and you're dead!" barked Wolf.

Kevin was facing the adjoining room, with the invader to his right, and his instincts took over. His right hand was on the grip of his foil, and with a blur of motion he brought the blade up, from left to right, in a defensive movement called a parry six. His hands were exceedingly fast and the blade darted through the air and slammed into Wolf's gun hand in the blink of an eye.

Wolf shrieked in surprise and pain and his gun went flying. The strike had been so ferocious and precise that if Kevin had been holding a real sword, Wolf's severed hand would have been flying through the air along with his weapon. As it was, his hand was severely injured and possibly even broken.

Rachel hadn't been bullied for some time, but her ability to conquer her fear and her tenacious street-fighting skills were still fully intact. The moment the gun was out of Wolf's hand she stepped from behind the door and kicked him between the legs with all of her might. Wolf fell backwards into his partner who had been entering the room behind him and they both went down in a tangled heap on the floor. Wolf's hand throbbed in agony and he had to fight to keep from vomiting from Rachel's well-targeted attack.

Rachel slammed the adjoining door shut and turned the dead-bolt lock back into place with a flick of her fingers.

"Quick, let's get out of here," said Ben, already moving toward the door to the outside. He snatched his cell phone from the end table beside him and slipped it into his pocket as he frantically began unlocking the door and removing the chain. Kevin's heart jackhammered so powerfully against his chest it was difficult for him to even breathe, and his two friends were affected the same way.

"What about Dad and Coach?" croaked Kevin, still clutching his foil as he and Rachel reached the door.

Rachel had seen the other room through the open door. "Not there," she said worriedly.

Kevin didn't know whether to be horrified or relieved at this bit of news, but he didn't have time to think about it further.

The three fencers sprinted from the room and around the corner of the motel, well aware that they had a five or ten second head-start, at most, on their attackers. As fast as they raced, their hearts continued to race even faster.

What in the world was going on?

CHAPTER 15

"If suffering brings wisdom, I would wish to be less wise."

—Ezra Pound, Poet, Fencing Enthusiast

As they raced around the corner of the motel they realized they were in more trouble than they had thought. The roof of the long, flat building extended over a concrete sidewalk that encircled the motel, and a single dim light bulb hanging down from a socket in the overhang was all that illuminated the backside of the structure. The lone bulb only allowed them to see about twenty yards into the pitch-blackness of the night, and they didn't like what they saw behind the motel—nothing but empty desert. No people and no cover of any kind. They would be sitting ducks for their heavily armed pursuers.

Kevin slammed on the brakes and his two friends were just able to follow suit before crashing into him.

Kevin's mind raced. They had seconds at most. If they could somehow make it through the lighted area and into the all-enveloping darkness beyond they would be safe. And while they would only be able to see a few feet ahead, guided by the faint light of a crescent moon, their pursuers wouldn't be able to see them at all.

Think! he ordered himself. He had considerable experience making split-second decisions on the field of battle, even if the battles were computer simulated. And he had an uncanny instinct for quickly choosing winning tactics and strategies. It was time to bring this ability into real life.

An idea flashed into his mind. If he launched a small stone into the lot in the opposite direction from where they were heading, he might be able to throw off their pursuit. Meanwhile, he and his friends could rush through the lighted section of desert and into the concealing darkness.

But it was too late! Before he could implement his plan, Dimitri rounded the back corner of the motel. After Dimitri had finally untangled himself from his hairy partner, he had only waited for Wolf for a few seconds before deciding to leave him on the floor of the room, writhing in pain.

But just as Dimitri came into view and began to bring his gun to bear on the three easy targets, Kevin seized upon a better idea, and this time acted on it instantly. Kevin was still holding his sword and stabbed fiercely at the uncovered light bulb above his head. He was rewarded by the sound of shattering glass, and the back of the motel was plunged into total darkness.

The mercenary chasing the three fencers screamed a curse as they suddenly disappeared from his view, just as surely as if a blindfold had materialized over his eyes. Rounding up a few kids should have been ridiculously easy. What was going on? His lip curled up in rage and frustration. Who *were* these kids?

"Move!" whispered Kevin to his friends. He dropped his foil on the concrete walkway and set off blindly into the desert, pulling Rachel and Ben with him. Realizing they needed to maintain physical contact until their eyes adjusted, the three friends scurried awkwardly across the desert, desperate to put as much distance between themselves and the man behind them as they possibly could.

Dimitri considered going after them, but he realized without a flashlight or proper equipment it would be foolish. He had no choice but to swallow his pride and report back to Diego.

The three kids continued to make steady progress for several minutes as they fought their growing panic. They had driven around the area earlier and knew their motel wasn't completely isolated from civilization. But stumbling about, nearly blind, it was easy to imagine this was the case. Surely any minute they would spot light from a road or an apartment complex or a gas station. But when?

Kevin expected a flashlight or car headlights to sweep the area any minute as their pursuers searched for them. He whispered to his friends to be ready to drop to the ground if any such beams approached.

When they had put about ninety yards behind them, Ben directed his friends to stop and pulled the cell phone from his pocket. If there was ever a time to call 9-1-1, this was it.

Kevin's heart skipped a beat as he realized that the light from the phone would stand out like a beacon in the desert, pinpointing their location. But just as he opened his mouth to whisper a warning, Ben slipped the phone under his black t-shirt and covered the screen with his other hand as it came to life. He had understood the danger as well.

There were no fools in this group, thought Kevin. If he had to be running for his life with two other kids, he couldn't ask for better company. Despite their intense fear and the staggering pressure they were all under, they continued to think clearly and act decisively. But then he shouldn't have been surprised. These were the very traits that helped make them such exceptional fencers, after all.

Ben peeked at his phone, uncovering it for just a second. With a look of disgust he quietly flipped it closed and slipped it back into his pocket. "No signal," he whispered in disappointment, so softly he was difficult to hear even a foot away. "Let's move."

What horrible luck, thought Kevin. They had all used cell phones to check in with their families back home within the past few hours and none of them had encountered any problems with signal strength.

They continued moving through the desert for several minutes, relieved at the lack of search beams or pursuit.

"Stop!" barked a deep voice coming from the curtain of darkness ten or fifteen yards behind them.

All three kids nearly jumped out of their skin.

Where had this guy come from? True, the man was beyond their current range of vision, but they had been listening to their surroundings intently and hadn't had the slightest warning of his approach. And how did he know where *they* were?

Recovering from their shock, they moved as a unit as quickly and quietly as they could. But as fast as they moved, the man behind them moved faster, because the next time they heard his voice it was unmistakably closer. "The game is up," he called out calmly in the still night. "I'm wearing night vision goggles. While you're nearly blind, I can see perfectly," he boasted.

Kevin shook his head miserably. If the man really did have night vision equipment they had no other choice but to surrender. But he might be bluffing. "What kind of night vision goggles?" asked Kevin as they continued moving away.

The man laughed. "Good," he said approvingly. "Testing to see if I'm bluffing. You know, you're beginning to impress me, kid. And not much does. You're gutsy *and* smart. If I was any less well prepared you might have even made it."

"I still didn't hear an answer," said Kevin into the darkness.

There was another round of laughter. "Okay," he said. "They're military grade. State of the art. They don't amplify light, they use advanced thermal imaging technology. Cryogenically cooled, of course." He paused. "Satisfied, or do I have to shoot one of you to prove I can see?"

Kevin signaled his friends to halt. They both knew that Kevin knew almost everything about military equipment. The man's answer must have been convincing. They stopped and stared defiantly into the night in the direction from which the voice was coming.

"Good," said the man pleasantly. "I didn't want to have to shoot one of you. My colleague Dimitri, whom you've met—the one *without* the broken hand and um . . . *groin* injury—will be here any minute with an SUV. I'll expect your full cooperation. If you offer even the slightest additional resistance," he added, his voice now taking on a cruel and menacing tone, "I won't hesitate to put a bullet between your eyes." He paused to let this sink in. "Are we clear?"

"What did you do with the two men in the adjoining room?" demanded Kevin.

"They were tranquilized and taken to a different location. I assure you, Kevin, your father and Coach Bryant are perfectly fine."

A cold chill ran down Kevin's spine. *The man had used their names. He knew exactly who they were.* For some reason, this was even more alarming than his threats.

"Who *are* you?" said Ben.

"Call me Diego."

Kevin had thought he'd detected a slight Spanish accent when the man spoke, and this name confirmed it.

"Think of us as just a friendly band of mercenaries," continued Diego in amusement. "Ex-Special Forces soldiers from around the world who've each decided to go into business for ourselves."

"What is this all about?" demanded Rachel.

"All in good time, Rachel," he said icily. "All in good time."

They could hear an SUV approaching them across the short span of desert they had just crossed. Its headlights were turned off, which could only mean the driver was using night-vision equipment as well.

They may have eluded these men briefly, but Kevin knew they were up against a team of commandoes that couldn't be more professional—or more dangerous. But he did have one card left to play. "You'd better leave us and get out of here right now," he said firmly. "We called 9-1-1 on a cell phone, you know. The cops will be here any second."

This time Diego laughed the loudest of all. "You are truly impressive, kid. You really are. You remind me of me." He shook his head. "Good try, but I know you're bluffing. First, if you really *had* called 9-1-1, the *last* thing you would do is tell me about it and put me on guard. Second, I have a device in the SUV that jams cell phone signals for about a half-mile radius. It's been on since this operation began."

"I don't believe you," said Rachel. "Why would you do that?"

"I wanted to be sure none of you happened to be blabbering into a cell phone when we came calling. Couldn't risk any of you getting off a warning before you were captured."

This time, Kevin knew in his heart the man was not bluffing. This would explain why Ben had been unable to get a signal when it had not been a problem a few hours before.

They had thought of everything! *What are we up against here?* Kevin thought in shock. These men were unbelievably careful, thorough, and prepared.

A sick feeling grew in the pit of Kevin Taylor's stomach, and for the first time he began to wonder if they had any hope of getting out of this alive.

CHAPTER 16

"Thus those skilled in war subdue the enemy's
army without battle . . . they conquer by strategy."
—Sun Tzu, *The Art of War*

The three prisoners traveled in silence in the middle row of the
large SUV. Diego drove, still wearing a gray wig and still made
up as an elderly man. Dimitri and Wolf watched the three prisoners like hawks from the third row of seats. Wolf had recovered—
mostly— from Rachel's kick, but his hand was now heavily ban-
daged and would take some time to fully heal. He glared at Kevin
and Rachel with such absolute hatred that they could almost feel
his eyes boring into the backs of their heads.

Diego had frisked them before they entered the SUV but found
nothing other than some loose change and Ben's cell phone, which
he quickly removed and pocketed. Interestingly enough, Diego
had driven back to the motel and had loaded their luggage into
the back of the SUV, including all three fencing bags. Even more
interesting, he had sent Wolf to retrieve the foil Kevin had left
at the back of the motel. Diego had then carefully stowed it in
Kevin's fencing bag.

The kids tried to get information from their abductors but
Diego would have none of it. At their first utterance he demanded

they remain silent for the rest of the drive or he would see to it that they became permanently incapable of speaking.

They traveled for about forty-five minutes; the last few miles on a wide gravel road that cut through the desert and its sporadic covering of sagebrush and cactus. Finally, they arrived at a large, two-story house with a three-car garage. Whoever had built it had truly prized their privacy. The gravel road continued on for as far as they could see, leading to a smattering of other homes, but these looked as tiny as Monopoly houses in the distance, and the nearest one was probably a quarter-mile or more away.

The house had smooth stucco siding, arches around the entryway and windows, and a Spanish style roof of red clay tiles. Two large air-conditioning units adorned the side of the house. They had doubtlessly been churning away most of the day but were finally at rest now that the night air had cooled to a pleasant seventy degrees.

Diego pressed a remote and the garage door slowly slid open to reveal Coach Bryant's yellow van. Its presence here was an eerie reminder of the nightmarish events of the past hour. Their captor pulled the SUV next to the van and jumped out.

"Follow me," said Diego as he entered the house from inside the garage. Dimitri held his gun on the three prisoners while Wolf shoved them forward forcefully, grinning as they slammed into each other, barely keeping their balance.

They entered the dwelling and were immediately struck by how barren it was. Not a single piece of art or a single framed photograph hung on the uniformly white walls. The few built-in bookshelves they passed were completely devoid of books or knickknacks. Makeshift curtains, all an ugly brown, were drawn at each window. The rooms didn't contain a single lamp or piece of furniture. The only exception was a small office whose door was open when they passed. And even this room only contained a chair and steel folding table, on top of which rested nothing but a computer and a phone.

The house was empty but it was not newly built. The original owners must have moved out and taken all their belongings with them. Diego, or whoever was in charge, must have decided the house fit their needs and bought it to serve as a base of operations—with no intention of ever living there.

Diego stopped just before entering the living room and motioned for the kids to enter in front of him.

Kevin gasped! Two bodies were laid out like cord-wood on the soft beige carpeting, impossible to miss in a room without furniture.

Kevin rushed over to his father and knelt down, ignoring the guns trained on his back. He studied him in horror. Had Diego lied when he had said they were okay! As Kevin saw the tiny rise and fall of his father's chest a powerful wave of relief washed over him. His dad was breathing! And so was Coach Bryant. Only then did Kevin realize that he had been holding his own breath, and inhaled loudly.

"As you can see," said Diego as Kevin stood and faced him, "both men are alive and in perfect health." His voice became decidedly more threatening and his upper lip curled into a sneer as he added, "How long this continues to be the case is entirely up to you and your two friends."

"What do you want?" snapped Kevin defiantly.

"Why nothing," he replied innocently. "For now. Right now all I want is for you to get some sleep. After all, you have a big day of fencing tomorrow."

Kevin shook his head in disbelief. "You've got to be kidding, right? You can't possibly still want us to compete in the tournament?" But as he said it he remembered they had gone out of the way to retrieve his backup foil and all the fencing gear at the motel.

"Oh, but I do," said Diego. "In fact, I'll be right there with you to root you on."

"Impossible," said Ben. "They'll never let you on the base."

"That remains to be seen," said Diego, amused.

Rachel frowned deeply. "I'll ask again," she said. "What is this all about?"

"And I will tell you again, as you American kids like to say, 'that's for me to know and you to find out.' Rest assured I will give you instructions whenever they are required." Diego paused. "But here are the general ground rules," he continued, glaring at them icily. "You don't try to resist. You don't try to run. You don't try to get help or try to sabotage my plans. Why? Because I will kill the two men lying here the instant I even *suspect* one of you is up to something. The only way these men survive—*the only way*—is if my plan succeeds."

"What if we cooperate but your plan fails anyway?" asked Kevin.

"Then your father and coach die," replied Diego matter-of-factly. "Were you not paying attention? If you ever want to see them alive again, you and your friends need to put as much energy into helping me succeed as you did into eluding my men."

Diego led them upstairs and into a large bedroom. Wolf trailed a few paces behind, holding a gun in his left hand, and remained just outside the doorway as the rest of the group entered. As they had come to expect, the room was bare except for three brand new sleeping bags rolled up neatly against one wall.

"This is where you'll be staying until I come for you tomorrow. I'll have your suitcases brought up." Diego pointed to a door inside the room. "You have your very own bathroom and shower, so you'll have no need to leave this room."

Kevin's eyes darted around the empty room, taking it in. The walls were smooth and uniform, broken only by a large window, the door to the bathroom, and a small air-conditioning vent high on one wall. Light blue carpeting covered the entire floor, except for another small air-conditioning duct in the corner of the room, covered by a metal grill. Brown drapes were closed over the room's only window.

Kevin thought they might be able to use the drapes to lower themselves from the window to the ground. But if Diego was telling the truth, escape wasn't enough. If they didn't also come up with a foolproof plan to free the coach and his father, both of these men would be killed in cold blood.

Diego studied Kevin as though he were an interesting and unusual lab specimen. "If you're as clever as I think you are," he said, reading Kevin's mind, "then you're already considering escape combined with a rescue attempt. So know this: opening that window will trigger an alarm. And when we leave you, we will turn on an ultrasonic motion detector in the hallway." He turned to look at Ben and Rachel. "Do you know how these devices work?"

They both looked blank.

"Kevin, why don't you explain it to your friends."

"I have no idea," said Kevin.

A look of contempt came over Diego's face. "If that's true, the money I spent on computer hackers was wasted, and that would put me in a very bad mood," he said gravely. "A bad enough mood to make me want to hurt your father. So why don't you reconsider your answer, *StabbingDude.*"

A cold chill went down Kevin's spine. StabbingDude was his online identity in the Internet military strategy game he played. If Diego was trying to intimidate Kevin by letting him know just how thorough his preparations had been, it was working.

"Okay," acknowledged Kevin. "Maybe I do know a bit about this type of motion detector after all. They send out ultrasonic sound waves," he said. "And measure how long it takes for the waves to bounce off every wall and corner and return. If anything—or anyone— blocks these waves, this timing is thrown off and an alarm sounds."

"Very good," said Diego. "I knew you wouldn't disappoint me."

Diego reached down and gripped the brass knob on the door to their room, preparing to shut it. "Escape is impossible," he said, addressing all three of them. "So get some sleep. I don't want to hear a single sound or a single voice. If the motion alarm is triggered for any reason," he added, gesturing to his hairy, injured colleague, "I'll give my friend Wolf here free reign to punish you as he sees fit."

He shook his head gravely. "And trust me, that wouldn't be good for your health. I have a funny feeling that he doesn't like you very much."

CHAPTER 17

"The opportunity of defeating the enemy is provided by the enemy himself."

—Sun Tzu, *The Art of War*

The tall Asian mercenary named Ahn brought up their luggage and then left them alone, making a show of arming the ultrasonic motion detector affixed to the wall in the corridor before he did.

"Any guesses as to what's going on here?" whispered Ben as they each unrolled identical bright red sleeping bags and slid inside.

Kevin quickly put a finger to his lips. "*Careful,*" he mouthed. "*Room might be bugged.*"

Their captors might be cruel and evil men, but they weren't stupid. Especially Diego. He was painstakingly thorough, impeccably trained and never seemed to miss a trick. Night-vision goggles. A device that could disrupt cell phone reception. Ultrasonic motion detectors. Planting a bug in their room would be par for the course.

"*Hold on,*" mouthed Rachel excitedly. She rooted around in her suitcase and pulled out a small pad of paper and pen she had packed and handed them to Kevin. He nodded in thanks.

This has to be about Nellis, he wrote. *Diego wants to use us somehow to help him get on base,* he scribbled hastily.

"*How?*" mouthed Rachel.

Kevin shrugged and shook his head in frustration.

Ben picked up the pad and wrote, *Why us? Could it have been anyone visiting Nellis tomorrow? Or did it have to be a fencer? And could it have been any fencers? Or are we special for some reason?*

Kevin took the pad. *None of this has been random,* he scribbled. *I'm sure of it. This guy, and this team, are pros. StabbingDude is my Internet gaming name. He really did hire computer hackers to track us on the Internet. So we weren't just unlucky. They targeted us for some reason."*

Rachel took the pad and was about to start writing when a familiar melody burst into the room so clearly it could have originated there. It was the flourish of music made by certain computers when they were first booted up.

The sound was coming from the corner of the room. From the air-conditioning vent in the floor!

The three fencers slid quietly toward the duct on their stomachs—still inside their sleeping bags—until their heads were within a few feet of it. One of the mercenaries must have turned on the computer in the office. While the office was not directly under them—in fact, was at the opposite end of the house—the air-conditioning ducts funneled the sound to them with nearly perfect clarity. The sound carried so well, in fact, they could even hear the clack of the keyboard as the mercenary began typing.

The door to the room opened with a brief, telltale creak.

"Welcome," said the man at the keyboard with a slight German accent. "It's nice to see you looking like yourself again. Not that you didn't make an intimidating senior citizen," he continued in amusement. There was a pause. "I heard you ran into a little trouble at the motel."

"Nothing we couldn't handle, my friend," said a voice the eavesdroppers immediately recognized as belonging to Diego. He shut the door. "Wolf just had some bad luck. He burst into the kids' room when Kevin Taylor was holding his sword."

"I heard the kid disarmed him."

"That's right."

"Even if the kid was lucky enough to be holding something he could use as a weapon when Wolf entered, that's quite an accomplishment. Wolf's reflexes are outstanding. The kid's hands must be as fast as we had hoped."

"It seems that way, Klaus," said the Cuban. "Tonight was very encouraging. The one thing we weren't sure of is if the kids would freeze under pressure. No need to worry about that anymore. When they were attacked, they could not have handled themselves any more impressively. Maybe *too* impressively."

"Meaning what?" said the man the tall Cuban had just called "Klaus".

Diego sighed loudly. "Meaning I think I should only bring two of the kids to Nellis tomorrow. With three of them and one of me, they might feel emboldened. There's more chance of them trying to be heroes. Trying something foolish."

"But it's not just you. We have others planted at the tournament," pointed out Klaus.

"Even so, I don't want us to have to keep tabs on *three* of them. Not as gutsy and resourceful as these kids are."

"I trust you explained to them what would happen to their adult traveling companions if we are not successful," said Klaus.

"I did," replied Diego gravely. "But I can't be sure they truly believe me."

"Why wouldn't they? It's absolutely true."

"Truth or non-truth doesn't matter. It's what they *believe* that matters. I think they'll cooperate. But I say we keep Ben Chang behind with the two adult hostages. This will make the situation at the tournament more manageable. It will also add to our leverage over Kevin and Rachel."

Upstairs, next to the air-conditioning vent, Ben Chang gulped. He would have preferred to attend the tournament where he would be surrounded by other people and where at least he would have the illusion of freedom and safety. Kevin and Rachel glanced at their friend worriedly but quickly turned their attention back to what was being said in the office downstairs. This vent—this express tunnel of sound—was providing them with a perfect opportunity to learn what was going on and they didn't want to miss even a single word.

"But Ben was a backup," complained Klaus. "In case Kevin lost before we needed him."

"That's a price I'm willing to pay. Kevin's the better fencer, and I've seen him in action. He won't lose. Not with his father's life on the line, he won't."

What did that mean? Kevin thought in horror. Were they serious? Could his winning at fencing really be *that* important to them?

"You know," said Klaus. "It occurred to me today that the Black Operations group calls the offensive version of Heaven's Shield, *The Devil's Sword*. Meanwhile, our strategy for stealing it relies on a *fencing* tournament. An interesting coincidence, don't you think?"

Diego laughed. "This just occurred to you *now*?" he said in amusement. Without waiting for Klaus to respond he continued on a serious note once again. "How are things going at your end?"

"Everything is on schedule. Mikah is truly a genius with computers. He was able to get Heaven's Shield to upload the software that we, um . . . borrowed . . . from the Black Ops group. It's poised and ready."

"So all we need now are the primary satellite command codes to take over, correct?"

"Correct."

"Mikah is absolutely positive we don't need to send the command codes from the American's control center?"

"He's positive. We can upload them from here. Once we do, he's set up software that will enable us to change the codes to those of our choosing, locking out the Americans forever. At that point we will own the system. Then all that's left to do is activate the hardware that will turn Heaven's Shield into The Devil's Sword."

"You have done well, my friend," said the Cuban.

"It's your end I'm worried about."

"My plan will go flawlessly," insisted Diego.

"I don't doubt it. I'm just not sure we'll get the command codes even if it does. You know truth drugs are likely to fail. We're talking about the key scientist on the team. The Americans have almost certainly conditioned him to resist these drugs. True, we could break his conditioning if we had weeks or months, but we don't. Within two or three hours—at most—they'll discover he's gone and change the codes."

"We'll try the truth drugs anyway, just in case we get lucky," said Diego. "But as you well know, my friend," he continued irritably, annoyed that he was being challenged, "my plan *does* assume these drugs won't work."

"I realize that. But assuming they fail, we have to rely on him giving us the Heaven's Shield command codes of his own free will. I don't think he'll do it. I don't care what's at stake for him personally."

"Don't be so pessimistic, my friend. You didn't think we'd get the Black Ops software either, and we did that. He'll give us the command codes. I have studied him extensively and I have never been more certain of anything. While I suspect he would hold out even under the most ruthless torture, I have identified his Achilles' heel. I'm sure of it."

"I hope you're right, Diego," said Klaus grimly. "I really hope you're right."

CHAPTER 18

"The belief in a supernatural source of evil is not necessary; men alone are quite capable of every wickedness."

—Joseph Conrad, Novelist

Kevin, Rachel and Ben stayed up for another hour, communicating with each other using Rachel's note pad. In the end, they decided their best strategy was no strategy at all. They would cooperate fully—at least for now. While they now had some hints as to what this was all about, they still knew almost nothing. Diego and Klaus were after someone. A man who knew command codes they needed to steal a weapon. But who? And how would they get him? Was he a fencer? Why was it so critical that Kevin win his bouts? Who were the others they had planted at Nellis?

With lives on the line and without the answers to these questions, their situation was truly hopeless. The best they could do was keep their eyes open and their minds active. Until they figured out exactly what they were up against, anything they tried was just as likely to worsen the situation as to improve it.

Finally, at one in the morning, exhausted, they settled into a fitful night's sleep.

At eight o'clock sharp they were awakened by a loud rap at the door. Kevin was rubbing sleep from his eyes as the door opened a few seconds later.

Coach Bryant stood calmly at the door, alone.

Adrenaline surged through Kevin's sleepy body and his pulse surged. The coach had escaped! But where was his father?

"Wipe those stupid looks off your faces and get up!" the coach barked at the three kids.

Only it wasn't the coach. It was Diego!

Upon closer inspection it was obvious. But *only* upon closer inspection. Diego's disguise was remarkable. He was thinner and a little taller than the coach, but he had chosen clothing that seemed to add just enough bulk to his frame to mimic the coach's weight and minimize their height difference. The mercenary's gray, lifeless eyes were now covered by pale blue contact lenses, precisely matching those of Coach Bryant, and he wore an identical mustache. While the facial structures of the two men were not alike, Diego had altered his slightly through the subtle use of makeup. And given how perfectly he had managed to copy Coach Bryant's wavy, jet-black hair, he was a close enough match to be the coach's identical twin.

It was now clear how Diego planned to bring them through Nellis security. He had done an impeccable job of disguising himself as an elderly man, and now this. Diego was as talented at the art of mimicry as even the most accomplished make-up artists in Hollywood.

The Cuban stepped into the room, and two mercenaries who had been out of sight behind him took up positions on either side of the door, their guns drawn. Diego walked over to the sleeping bag Ben was in and stood over him. "You're coming with me," he said sternly. "Let's go."

Ben squinted his eyes in pretend confusion. He didn't want to give Diego even the slightest reason to suspect they had overheard his conversation with Klaus the night before. "Why me?" protested Ben. "You said we were all going to the tournament together."

"Plans have changed," snapped Diego.

The fact that this ruthless killer was now the spitting image of the coach they admired continued to be unsettling to all of the prisoners.

"I won't leave my friends," insisted Ben.

"This is not a discussion!" thundered Diego. "In exactly ten seconds I'm going to stomp on this sleeping bag with all of my weight. Whether you're in it at the time is entirely up to you. Ten . . . nine . . . eight—"

Ben scrambled out of the bright red bag and was on his feet by the time the Cuban reached three.

"It seems that you are able to move quickly, after all," said Diego coldly.

"Where are you taking him?" asked Rachel worriedly.

"He's joining your other two companions as a hostage."

As he said this a shorter man entered the room, one the kids had not seen before. He was wearing a short-sleeved shirt and looked like a weight-lifter. "Sorry to interrupt your babysitting chores, Diego," said the man in amusement, "but I wanted to take a look at you before you left."

All three prisoners recognized the voice and accent immediately. It was Klaus.

Klaus studied his partner carefully, reaching out to adjust Diego's wig by a fraction of an inch. "Not perfect, but good enough," he said. "Good luck," he added and then strode briskly from the room and down the stairs, returning to whatever it was he had been doing.

Diego led Ben away down the corridor. Less than a minute later another mercenary arrived and delivered Kevin and Rachel's fencing clothing, including the hard plastic chest-protectors that many fencers wore under their jackets during a tournament. "You have exactly thirty minutes to be ready," said the soldier as he left the room, closing the door noisily behind him.

Kevin noted with interest that the mercenaries had not yet given them their foils. After last night, perhaps they were not eager to put swords, blunt as they were, in the hands of those who were well trained in their use.

Kevin and Rachel took turns in the bathroom, showering and brushing their teeth, and finished dressing just as Diego came to retrieve them. They were marched downstairs and into the living room, wearing white fencing clothing from head to toe.

Kevin's father, the coach, and Ben Chang were seated on three metal folding-chairs, their hands cuffed behind them to small steel rungs the mercenaries had installed the night before in the far wall. Kevin began to move toward his father but was pulled back, hard, by the soldier closest to him. "Stay put!" he ordered.

Mr. Taylor inspected his son anxiously. Thankfully, both he and Rachel appeared to be unharmed. A look of astonishment came over his face as his gaze left his son and fell upon Diego for the first time. When Ben had joined the two adults as a hostage he had quickly filled them in about the conversation they had overheard through the AC vent, and told them that Diego was impersonating the coach, but Mr. Taylor wasn't prepared for just how good of a job the Cuban had done. His resemblance to the coach was *uncanny*. As for Coach Bryant, he looked horrified as he stared at a funhouse-mirror reflection of himself.

Kevin's father tore his eyes from Diego and returned his attention to his son. "Ben tells me you and Rachel are holding up pretty well," he said.

"So far," said Kevin. "What about you and Coach Bryant?"

"We're okay," said his father. "The tranquilizer they used doesn't seem to have caused any harmful after effects." He stared worriedly into his son's eyes. "Kevin," he continued, "Ben told us about what happened at the motel. How you all tried to fight these guys off. I'm proud of your courage, Kevin. I really am. And yours Rachel. But you took a big chance. These men are cold-blooded killers and they're in the driver's seat. It's best to cooperate."

"Bravo," said Diego, clapping lightly. "You should listen to your father. Cold-blooded killers," he added in amusement. "I like that." He snapped his fingers at his men and gestured toward the three hostages. "Tape their mouths shut," he ordered, obviously not interested in anything else they might have to say.

Diego glared at Kevin and Rachel as his men tore pieces of gray duct tape from a roll and went to work silencing the prisoners. "So let's review the game plan one more time before we leave," he said. "You will both do as I say. Quickly, wholeheartedly and without questions. Is that understood?"

"Understood," they both mumbled in unison.

"Good. Here is how things are going to work. If I give you an order and you don't carry it out *immediately*—and with gusto— my men chop off one finger from each of the hostages with a pair of pruning shears." He raised his eyebrows. "In a way, I almost hope this happens in the early going so I can prove I'm not bluffing."

"How will this prove it?" asked Rachel in disgust. "We'll be at the tournament. How will we know what you did or didn't do to the hostages?"

Diego smiled happily, glad that she had asked the question. "Oh, but you will, Rachel, you will. I'll make sure of that. My colleagues will take digital pictures of their newly deformed hands and send them to me on my cell phone for your enjoyment."

Rachel shrank back in horror. This man was a true monster.

"Note that after I disfigure the hostages, I will still have them as leverage. This is only the penalty for not carrying out my orders with 110 percent effort. If you actively *oppose* me, the penalty increases. My men will kill one of the hostages and send me a picture of their bloody corpse for your viewing pleasure. And then, guess what, I still have two hostages left as leverage. Does this help clarify the situation for you?"

Both of them confirmed that it did.

"Good. Do as you're told, and do it well, and all of you will get through this unharmed."

Kevin frowned deeply. "How do we know you won't kill us all anyway when you're done?"

"You don't," said Diego bluntly. "The only thing you know for sure is that I *will* kill you if you cross me. But if it makes you feel any better, when I have what I want, there would be no point in killing you. And I'm a man of my word. I've told you I'll let you all go, unharmed, and I will."

"Even though we can identify you?" said Kevin skeptically.

Diego laughed. "Do you *want* me to kill you?" he said in disbelief. He shook his head. "You only *think* you can identify me. Klaus and I change appearances as easily as other men change clothing. Your government has been after us for years and hasn't gotten close."

Kevin watched Diego intently as he answered. If Kevin became convinced they would all be killed no matter what happened he would need to dramatically alter his strategy. But Diego's answer had been reasonable and had been given without hesitation. There was a chance he was telling the truth.

Kevin caught Rachel's eye and give her a very small, but very meaningful, nod. She looked as though she had just swallowed a cup full of foul-tasting medicine, but reluctantly returned the nod.

"Okay," said Kevin. "We'll cooperate. But I have to be able to talk to my dad to make sure everyone is okay every once in a while."

"Of course," said Diego smoothly, as if he were the most reasonable man in the world. "A fair request. And one I knew you would make. My men will call periodically and put your dad on the phone so you can confirm the hostages haven't been harmed."

Kevin nodded.

"We have to go now," said Diego. He turned to the hostages. "Stay healthy," he said with a smirk.

He began to walk briskly toward the garage and his men prodded Kevin and Rachel to follow.

A tear came to Kevin's eye. He knew he might never see any of the three hostages alive again. "I love you, Dad," he shouted over his shoulder, fighting to keep his voice strong. "We won't let you down," he added with determination, knowing that his father's mouth was taped firmly shut and he was unable to respond.

Soon they had boarded Coach Bryant's yellow fencing van and were on the road. Diego had insisted that both Kevin and Rachel cram in the front seat with him so he could keep better track of them. The Cuban stopped at a fast-food drive-through to order breakfast for the kids, but they were still able to reach Nellis in under an hour.

Several cars were in front of them at the main gate. While they awaited their turn, Diego turned to his passengers. "Here is your first chance to disrupt my plans," he told them. "When the guard comes over, one word from you and he'll detain me. After a little investigation I'll be imprisoned for life. Meanwhile, you two will be free and away from this mess. You'll both be heroes."

Kevin nodded, a scowl on his face. "And we'll never see my father, Coach Bryant, or Ben alive again," he said, anticipating Diego's next words.

"Glad to see you're catching on. That is correct. My men will butcher them like hogs. But it's your choice. There is nothing I can do to stop you."

"*We get it already!*" barked Kevin, fighting to control his growing rage. "You've made your point. Over and over and over again. We'll cooperate, okay."

"*You'd better believe you will!*" snarled Diego as the last car in front of them was finally waved ahead.

The Cuban took a deep breath to compose himself. He turned to his passengers and winked. "It's show-time," he said, his face now relaxed and friendly.

And with that, the tall Cuban drove the van the last few feet to the gatehouse.

CHAPTER 19

"Pressure makes diamonds."

—General George S. Patton

Aguard approached the van. He was not the same guard who had manned the gate the day before but he had the same weaponry and breed of dog, and the same well-pressed uniform and clean-cut appearance. He asked for identification and Diego calmly handed him Coach Bryant's driver's license.

Finally, after what seemed like an hour but was really only thirty seconds, the guard handed the license back and asked for the kids' names. He consulted his binder yet again and a quizzical look came over his face. "There should be two more visitors with you," he said. "A Ted Taylor and a Ben Chang."

"I'm afraid Ben came down with a nasty flu," explained Diego, shaking his head sympathetically. "Ted is staying behind at the motel to look after him."

His speech was slower than usual as he concentrated on sounding like a native-born American. Just as actors could put on convincing British or other accents for performances, Diego was doing a flawless impersonation of an American.

"You can strike them from the list if you like," added Diego. "They definitely won't be coming today."

"That's too bad," said the guard sincerely, making a note on one of the pages. A few minutes later he and the dog completed their inspection and he waved them through, reminding them they were required to remain in the gym at all times until they were prepared to leave the base. Diego seemed perfectly relaxed the entire time, as if it had never occurred to him there was any risk of being discovered.

They parked at the designated lot and entered the massive gymnasium. There was even more hustle and bustle inside the vast room than there had been the day before. Youth events comprised the vast majority of the Sunday schedule. White-clad kids of all ages and sizes scurried about purposefully in the gym like a swarming colony of ants. Scores of parents and coaches dotted the gym as well, dressed in casual clothing of all colors and varieties, along with several Nellis soldiers in uniform that had stopped in for the unique opportunity to watch the sport of fencing.

Diego surveyed the room for several long seconds. "Stay close to me," he said. "Pretend you're both on a one-foot leash." He no longer bothered to disguise his accent. "The first thing we need to do is notify the tournament organizers that Ben is withdrawing due to illness."

Upon hearing this, Kevin shot Rachel a worried look. Diego seemed incapable of missing an angle or making a mistake. If they were to have any hope of finding a way out of this, he needed to start.

Diego turned to Kevin. "Your instructions are as follows: just keep winning, at all costs, until I give you further orders. Lose and I kill the hostages. It's that simple." The clamor inside the gym was so unrelenting that Diego didn't even bother to lower his voice. "Is that understood?"

Even though Kevin had known this was coming after eavesdropping on Diego's conversation the night before, he shot the Cuban a look of disgust. "You're out of your mind," he said bitterly.

"That could be. But I'm also serious about this. *Deadly* serious."

"But this is ridiculous!" snapped Kevin in exasperation. "What does my fencing have to do with anything? How could winning be so important that you'd actually kill innocent people if I didn't? Why would you possibly care?"

"*Why* I care isn't important. All you need to know is that I do—and the penalty for failure. Now, I'll ask you again: do you understand my instructions and what's at stake?"

Kevin nodded miserably. "Yes," he said. "But even if I fence my brains out—even if I have the best day of my life—the competition here is brutal. How can I possibly be sure I'll win every bout?"

"That's your problem, not mine," said the Cuban coldly. "All I know is that you had better find a way."

Diego turned to Rachel. "Rachel, I know very little about fencing, so your job will be to do anything and everything you can to help Kevin win. I'm withdrawing you from your event along with Ben."

Rachel said nothing, but this was welcome news. She had wanted to stay with Kevin in case they learned enough to turn the tables on Diego. The last thing she wanted to do was pretend to care about fencing when their very survival was at stake.

They found an empty spot against the gymnasium wall to leave their fencing bags, and Diego withdrew Ben and Rachel from the tournament as planned.

As Diego led Kevin and Rachel through a heavy thicket of humanity, they remained hyper-alert, trying to spot anyone who might be watching them. They needed to identify Diego's allies as soon as they could. Kevin had thought they were being watched as they stood in line at the armorer's table the day before and he could well have been right. Diego may have been keeping tabs on them even then.

"Well if it isn't Scott Bryant," said a balding man they were passing, holding out his hand to Diego with a warm smile. "What are you doing out West, you old dog?"

Diego ignored the outstretched hand. "I'm afraid you've got the wrong guy," he said firmly, looking at the man as if he had lost his mind.

Upon hearing Diego's voice and taking a closer look the man withdrew his hand in embarrassment. "Sorry about that," he said. "You look a lot like a guy I know," he added before continuing on his way.

Even though Coach Bryant had spent most of his career on the East Coast, Kevin had been sure at least a few people at the tournament would know him. He had wondered how Diego would handle this if they ran into one. Now he knew. Very simply and very smoothly. Diego had obviously rehearsed this response ahead of time. Only if someone knew Coach Bryant, and also that Kevin and Rachel were his students, would they get suspicious of such a close look-alike—and this wasn't about to happen.

A deep voice came over the loudspeaker, blasted at a high enough volume to be heard in the noisy gym. "Attention fencers and friends. The youth events are about to begin for the day. On behalf of Nellis Air Force Base we want to thank all competitors for their participation and sportsmanship. These fine young people represent what is best about our country, as does the sport of fencing. Control, speed, intelligence, sportsmanship; all exemplified by this most ancient of sports."

There was a brief pause and then the voice continued. "We are happy to report that Major General Ronald Alexander, the Commander of Nellis Air Force Base, will be here later this afternoon to watch several of the bouts. General Alexander was one of the most highly decorated fighter pilots in American history and was an All-American fencer at Ohio State University over thirty years ago. The General will be personally handing out medals to all of today's winners."

Kevin and Rachel traded a quick, meaningful glance. The commander of the entire base was coming! *This* was who Diego was after. It had to be. And the general would be awarding the medals, which explained why it was so important for Kevin to win. Diego must be planning to make his move—whatever it was—during the medal ceremony.

"Our first event of the morning," continued the announcer, "the boys' fourteen-and under foil, will begin in five minutes. Please listen carefully for your pool assignments." Seconds later the announcer began reading off groups of names along with their specific strip assignments.

Fencing tournaments typically had two phases, the pool phase and the direct elimination phase. During the pool phase the contestants were separated into a number of different groups. In this case, the sixty-four competitors were broken down into nine groups of fencers. All fencers in a given group would face off against all other fencers in that group in five-touch bouts. Wins, along with points for and against each fencer, would be carefully recorded. In this way the best fencers would begin to separate themselves from the pack.

Once the pool bouts were completed, the actual tournament would begin—the direct elimination phase. In this phase the bouts would be to fifteen touches and only the winners of each round would advance in the tournament. The results from the pool bouts were fed into a computer to determine the all-important seedings for this second phase. The top seeds, those fencers who had performed the best in the pools, would be scheduled to face the bottom seeds in the early rounds, and wouldn't meet other top seeds until much deeper in the tournament. Without such a system, the two best fencers at a tournament could meet in the very first round, with one of them being eliminated. *With* such a system in place, however, it was far more likely the top two fencers wouldn't meet until the finals, as it should be.

"Pool number five," continued the announcer. "Seth Bernstein, Roman Forcier, Miguel Padgitt, Kevin Taylor, Carl E. Saeks, Scott Lee, and Hunter Schatz. Please report to strip number seventeen."

Diego led Kevin and Rachel to strip seventeen, and soon thereafter the pool bouts began.

Kevin knew immediately that he was off his game. He was tired and he hadn't had a chance to warm up. With so many lives on the line, he found it nearly impossible to concentrate on fencing. To make matters worse, this was a higher-level tournament than he had competed in before, and there were no easy opponents—just as he had expected.

Kevin won his first pool bout five to three. In his second, he was down four to two and feeling helpless. His movements were slow and confused.

"What are you doing!" thundered Diego angrily from the sidelines when Kevin's opponent scored his fourth touch. "You know the price of failure!" he finished coldly.

Several spectators eyed Diego with distaste, objecting to this kind of negative coaching.

What an *idiot,* thought Rachel. Although she shouldn't be surprised that a ruthless killer would make a horrible coach. Kevin was already under so much pressure it was a wonder he wasn't gripping his sword so tightly that he couldn't move his arm. More pressure was the *last* thing he needed. "Kevin, just *relax,*" she shouted, loudly enough to be heard over the clashing of blades as Kevin and his opponent raced up and down the long strip. "You're *better* than this kid. He's got *nothing.* I've fenced you hundreds of times and I *know* you are. Now stay loose, settle down, and play your game."

This time most of the spectators shot a harsh look of disapproval at Rachel. She ignored this reaction, knowing she had earned it. It was bad form to openly belittle an opponent, but far too much was at stake for her to worry about ruffling feathers.

Kevin took a deep breath and began to settle down. Rachel was right. He *was* a better fencer than the kid he was facing. He just needed to play his game and be patient.

Within ninety seconds Kevin had tied the score. Then, with time running out, his opponent dropped down to a crouch and thrust his blade upward, hoping to catch Kevin off guard. Kevin parried the attack and then flicked his blade over his opponent's head as he crouched on the ground, striking the challenger on his exposed back in the middle of the words, "Padgitt" and "USA" stenciled in blue letters on his vest.

He had won! He was still undefeated.

Kevin won his next bout as well, but it was also closer than he would have liked. While he waited for his next bout to begin, Diego called his men and allowed Kevin to speak briefly with his father. Mr. Taylor reported that the hostages were all still in good health, which came as a huge relief to Kevin and Rachel.

Kevin was finally warming up and Rachel was helping him scout his opponents when he wasn't fencing. She also made sure he had an inexhaustible supply of Gatorade to replace the many quarts of sweat that would pour from his body throughout the event. While he would have given anything to have Coach Bryant there helping him, he and Rachel analyzed fencers well together and her input and coaching were quite valuable. Kevin ended the pool phase of the competition with six wins and no losses. Even so, most of his bouts had been very close and he knew his seeding would reflect this.

Forty minutes later the seeding and the tournament brackets had been finalized and taped to the wall at one end of the gym. Kevin was the seventh seed. He was worried that this wouldn't be high enough to satisfy Diego, but Diego was all smiles after he had studied the draw sheet. Apparently the tournament was shaping up to his liking.

If only Kevin and Rachel could say the same. They had made no progress in discovering what they were up against, or identifying any of Diego's accomplices—*if* they actually existed.

During the wait for the seedings, Kevin finally had some time to think. Was Diego's entire, elaborate plan dependent on the ability of a fourteen-year-old to win a medal? Kevin refused to believe it. The element of chance played too big a role in a competitive sporting event: there were too many ways he could lose. Even if he was the best fencer here, which he wasn't. Risking the entire plan on such an unpredictable outcome would be a big mistake—and Diego didn't make mistakes. He must have a backup strategy.

But even so, if Kevin failed and Diego was forced to go to his backup plan, he didn't doubt that Diego would still kill them all, even if the backup ultimately succeeded. Kevin had no choice but to assume that for every contest he fought, lives were hanging in the balance.

But could he keep winning?

He had slept poorly the night before and his nerves were shot. This tournament was the most challenging he had entered in his life and he was already beginning to tire.

No matter what was at stake, no matter how much he wanted to win, he knew in his heart it would take a miracle for him to reach the medal round.

And judging from the nightmarish events of last fourteen hours, miracles appeared to be in short supply.

CHAPTER 20

"Never, never, never give up."

—Winston Churchill

Kevin made it through the first direct elimination round easily, winning fifteen to three. His opponent in the next round was left-handed, which always made things more difficult since most of his experience was against righties. He ultimately won fifteen to ten, but the bout sapped considerable energy from him— energy he would need for later rounds when the competition was at its fiercest.

In the next round, the round-of-sixteen, he fell behind twelve to nine and Diego became more agitated by the second. Kevin forced himself to ignore the score. To ignore his growing fatigue. To ignore the life-and-death stakes. He emptied his mind and put himself into a fencing trance. His entire universe consisted of the movement of his opponent and his blade and nothing more.

It worked! Kevin only came out of his trance when he heard the referee announce he had won, fifteen to thirteen. He had truly dodged a bullet that time.

But how long could this continue? Although he was now one of only eight fencers still standing, he would need to win two more bouts to earn a medal.

Diego was elated by this victory more than any of the others. Kevin wasn't sure why, since he was now only in the quarterfinals, but Diego's mood had improved dramatically.

Diego escorted Kevin and Rachel to strip fourteen to scout Kevin's next opponent. This would be the winner of Gateway versus Sprowles. They arrived just as the bout was beginning. This was the first they had seen of Matt Gateway all day. Given their meeting and friendly conversation the day before, if none of this insanity had occurred, the *Excalibur* fencers would have sought him out and continued to be friendly with him. But Diego had kept them isolated and this hadn't come to pass.

Matt Gateway was as short and slight as Rachel, but Kevin knew from long experience that stature mattered very little in fencing. He needed to see Matt in action and was eager to do so.

The bout started and Kevin realized immediately that he was in big trouble. Matt Gateway had earned the number two seed in the tournament and this seed was clearly well deserved. He moved like a supercharged demon, and his bladework, footwork, and quickness were exceptional. Kevin began to feel ill as he watched him fence. Matt mixed up his game beautifully, and if he had a favorite parry or tactic Kevin was at a loss to identify it. The last thing Kevin needed was to have to face a kid who was as unpredictable as he was fast.

Gateway beat Sprowles with ease. The final score was fifteen to three. Fencers like Sprowles who were good enough to survive into the third round weren't supposed to be crushed so easily, thought Kevin in despair.

While Kevin waited for his quarterfinal match against Matt to begin, Diego handed him a phone. "You have ten seconds," he said.

"Dad?" said Kevin eagerly into the phone.

"Yeah. It's me, Kevin. Are you and Rachel okay?" asked his father, fighting to keep his voice strong.

"We're good. What about you?"

"We haven't been hurt." His father grunted as the phone was snatched away from him. "I love you Kevin," he shouted into the still-open phone as the connection was broken. This time, his father's voice was thick with emotion.

Kevin hastily pulled his fencing helmet over his head so no one could see the tears beginning to slide down his face. The situation was *hopeless*. He was going to lose, and he would never see his father again.

He shook his head sharply, fighting to get himself back under control. He could not allow himself to think like this. He removed the helmet and wiped his face with the back of his hand. If he wanted to have any chance of saving his father, he didn't have the luxury of despair. He needed to focus all of his energy on his next bout— and then some. Even then, he knew, he would have to fence the match of his life to come out on top. But he would not go down easily, he vowed. He would find a way to channel all his despair and fear into fierce determination.

Matt Gateway approached Kevin a few minutes before their bout was set to begin. Diego pretended not to care but watched the two boys intently from the corner of his eye. And he wasn't the only one. Kevin noticed the two men he had spotted near the armorer's table doing the same. But now it was clear: they hadn't been watching the kids from *Excalibur* the day before. They had been watching *Matt Gateway*.

But why? Who *was* he?

"Hey. What's up?" said Matt. "I can't believe we haven't run into each other more today. Where are your two friends?"

"Rachel's buying some Gatorade. And Ben—" Kevin glanced at Diego who glared at him icily. "Ben came down with the, ah . . . flu."

"Wow, that stinks," said Matt with a frown. "What bad luck." He paused for a few seconds and then with a warm, genuine smile added, "How come you didn't tell me you were so good yesterday?"

Kevin was taken aback. "Me?"

"Yes you," said Matt. "I've never heard of you before, but I watched one of your bouts. Let me tell you, Kevin, you've got skills."

"Thanks," said Kevin. He frowned deeply. "They're not so hot compared to yours, though," he added.

Matt grinned. "I've been doing this for five years," he reminded Kevin. "And I've been the top youth fencer in Nevada for eighteen months now. You've only been fencing for *two years,* and already you're one of the few kids in this tournament I'm worried about."

Kevin nodded numbly. In other circumstances, he would have been delighted by the compliment. Matt Gateway didn't need to be this friendly before their bout. Kevin had seen other fencers, not nearly as good, who carried themselves with arrogance and had nothing but disdain for their opponents. Matt was a really nice kid. But this changed nothing. Kevin *had* to find a way to beat him, no matter what it took.

Less than a minute later the referee called them both to the *on guard* line. The crowd for the bout was the biggest Kevin had seen. Several uniformed soldiers, who evidently knew Matt or his family, looked on intently. A short man in his forties who had the same facial features and slight body type as Matt was in the crowd as well— obviously his father.

Four of the spectators seemed out of place. The two men who had been spying on Matt and two others cut from the same mold. All wore casual clothing but there was something distinctly military about them. They didn't stand together, yet they were unmistakably linked. While everyone else in the crowd had their eyes on the fencers as they took the *on guard* line, they had their eyes *on the crowd.* And they were serious as death. It reminded him of something he had seen before.

A movie! It was a movie about a fictional president. That was it. These men looked and behaved exactly like the president's bodyguards had in the film.

Kevin didn't have time to consider this further as the referee called out, "On guard! Fencers ready. Fence!"

As the period began Kevin found a strength within himself he didn't know he had. His retreats were explosive. He avoided Matt's blade as if it were a striking rattlesnake that would deliver death with only a single successful attack. Which wasn't far from the truth. If he could play perfect defense, keep the score as close to zero as possible, perhaps he could frustrate Matt Gateway into making some mistakes.

The referee called a halt and Kevin shot a glance at Rachel, who often used hand gestures to give him tactical advice. But she wasn't even watching him. Diego was whispering in her ear at a furious pace, and her expression was grim and focused. He must be giving her detailed and complex instructions. But what could he possibly be telling her?

The three minute first round took a huge toll on Kevin. The moment the break was called he pulled off his mask and began downing the quart of red Gatorade Rachel had brought him in quick gulps. The score was two to one, Gateway.

As Kevin drank, Diego rushed over to his side and crouched down to whisper in his ear. "Change to your back-up foil," he instructed. "Then hit him in the leg immediately. Hard."

"What?" whispered Kevin in disbelief. "If you want me to win, why have me hit him off target? While I'm doing that, he'll have the chance to hit me *on* target."

"One more word and your father loses a finger," snapped Diego. "Use your back-up sword," he demanded. "Then immediately hit him hard in the leg. I don't care if you lose the point. Understood?"

Kevin nodded, dazed. "Understood," he mumbled lifelessly.

"Time!" announced the referee. "Fencers *en garde,*" he said.

Kevin quickly got the ref's attention, complaining that his handle was loose and asking to use his back-up weapon. The ref nodded, and Kevin retrieved his second foil where it had been lying beside the strip. The ref held the new foil so it was pointing straight up and placed a hollow, cylindrical weight on the tip, testing to make sure it didn't compress too easily. He nodded to Kevin to indicate this new weapon had passed and called once again for the fencers to return to the *on guard* line.

The moment the period started Kevin lunged forward to attack. Matt easily parried the thrust and buried the tip of his blade in Kevin's chest, while Kevin—who hadn't even *tried* to defend himself—continued moving forward, striking Matt hard on the upper thigh. Matt winced in pain but quickly shook it off. No one had any idea the off-target hit had been deliberate.

The ref recounted the action, awarding the touch to Matt. "Gateway leads, three touches to one," he finished.

Now two touches behind, Kevin turned to Diego and shook his head angrily, as if to say, "*Satisfied?*"

But from Diego's expression there was *no question* he was satisfied. In fact, he looked like the cat that ate the canary. He was trying to repress a triumphant smile but failing badly. Rachel, on the other hand, looked like death; pale and tight with tension.

Two minutes into the second round, Matt stumbled during a lunge and Kevin was able to hit him. When fencing resumed, Kevin charged at his opponent, but as Matt retreated he fell clumsily backwards onto the strip.

"Halt!" shouted the referee as Kevin held out his hand to help pull Matt Gateway back to his feet. Matt gave no indication that he even saw the outstretched hand. He didn't move an inch. In fact, he looked as if he had fallen unconscious.

Matt's father raced onto the strip. Three of the men Kevin suspected were bodyguards quickly surrounded the senior Gateway and his son in a protective cocoon. Matt's father called his name several times. When Matt didn't respond, his father gently removed his mask and shoved his fingers against the carotid artery in his son's neck to check his pulse. The crowd was breathless and the area around the strip became eerily silent.

"Is he okay?" asked the ref anxiously.

"He's breathing," said Dr. Gateway, his voice deep and gravelly. "But his breath is faint and his pulse is very low. And he's cold. He should be on fire given all the sweat that's pouring out of him."

"I just called over to the base hospital," announced Diego from the crowd, holding a cell phone and pretending to be a concerned spectator. "They said to drive him there immediately. They'll wait for him out front. I'll fill them in on his symptoms," he added.

One of the bodyguards looked at Matt's father who quickly nodded. Matt was light and the massive guard lifted him gently off the ground without much trouble. Everything was happening so quickly that Kevin's head was spinning.

Rachel rushed forward. "I know what happened to him," she said breathlessly. "The same thing happened to me a month ago. The same symptoms! It almost killed me!" she added, almost hysterically.

What? Kevin thought. She hadn't been sick in years. But then it hit him: she must be following Diego's instructions.

Matt's father turned to Rachel. "What was it?" he asked.

"A very rare bug. He's about to get far worse. In an hour or so blood will start coming from his nose and the corners of his eyes. I can tell the doctor all about the symptoms and what they did to save me if you want."

"Thanks," said Matt's father hurriedly. "Come with us," he added, already rushing to the nearest exit. Rachel and all four bodyguards—one of them carrying Matt—followed closely behind.

The moment the group left the building Diego casually walked past Kevin. "Go into the men's room in five minutes," he whispered

out of the corner of his mouth, continuing to walk and not looking at Kevin. "Stand at a sink and wash your hands," he added
before disappearing into the crowd.

The large group that had been watching the quarterfinal bout
was still abuzz over Matt Gateway's collapse. Kevin forced himself to put them out of his mind. He needed to calm down and
think! He only had a few minutes before Diego pulled on his leash
once again.

So what had happened to Matt? Why had he gone down? The
only conclusion possible was that Kevin's strike to his leg was
responsible. Diego had given Rachel her instructions *before* Matt
had collapsed. So he must have known it was coming. And Diego
had insisted Kevin use his back-up foil. This had to be the key.

Kevin leaned back against a nearby wall and examined his
weapon. There was no doubt it was one of the two he had brought.
He studied the tip but nothing looked out of the ordinary. He
placed the tip on top of the very end of one of his tennis shoes,
curled his toes in, and pressed down hard. He kneeled to examine
the shoe.

The tiniest of holes had been drilled through the leather! Sure
enough, Diego had rigged Kevin's foil during the night so it could
pass the weight test but still contained a retractable needle that
emerged when enough force was applied. No wonder Diego needed him to hit Gateway off target. Otherwise the needle would
have been stopped by the hard plastic chest-protector Matt wore
under his fencing jacket.

What had he injected into the poor kid? If it killed him, he
would be the murderer. An unknowing and unwilling murderer,
perhaps, but the instrument of Matt's death nonetheless. His
stomach churned and he felt like vomiting.

So this had been the real point to the entire exercise. This had
nothing to do with General Alexander after all. Diego had needed
Kevin to do well enough to face Matt Gateway and inject him

with something. But to what end? And who was this kid? Why did he have his own bodyguards? And what was Rachel's role in all this?

It was time to walk to the bathroom. As he did so, he continued to work on the puzzle, but didn't arrive at any further insights. He stood at the sink as he had been told, lost in thought, looking down at his hands as he washed them.

A man approached the sink next to his and turned on the water. "I'm leaving you now," said the man, not turning to look at Kevin. It was Diego!

The Cuban had been very busy during the past five minutes. His false mustache was now gone and he had a baseball cap over his black wig. He had removed his contact lenses and his eyes were now the same cold gray color they had been at first. He had made several other subtle changes as well. Someone who had stood next to him the entire day would no longer recognize him.

"Look down!" hissed Diego.

Kevin did as he was told.

A boy came out of a stall and began washing his hands at the next sink over. Diego waited patiently for him to leave and then said, barely loud enough for Kevin to hear, "Listen carefully, because I won't say this again. Now that Matt Gateway is out of the tournament, you're in the semifinals. You need to keep fencing. I put a cell phone in your fencing bag. Get it. My men will call this phone every half-hour so you can speak with your father. All you have to do is mind your own business and fence and you and everyone else gets out of this."

"What did you have me do to Matt?" demanded Kevin. "And what are you doing with Rachel?"

"All you need to know is that they'll both be fine as long as you do as you're told. I'm going to take a direct route out of here in your coach's van. You can have me stopped, but I think you know by now what a mistake that would be." He paused. "Remember the saying, 'he who knows when he can fight and when he cannot will be victorious.' Well, this is definitely a time when you can't fight. I still hold all the cards."

The saying Diego had quoted was quite familiar to Kevin, but his head was spinning from everything that was happening and he couldn't immediately place it. But it didn't matter. There were far more important matters at hand. His eyes narrowed. "Why take any chances with me at all? Why not just force me to come with you?"

Diego frowned. "You never stop calculating angles, do you kid?" he said irritably. "I'll tell you. Since you were fencing Matt Gateway when he went down, you've become famous within this gym. People know who you are and will now be taking note of your activities."

This explained why Diego had changed his appearance and was now being careful not to be seen speaking with him, thought Kevin.

"So anything else you do that's out of the ordinary will attract attention," continued Diego. "Like leaving the gym before your next bout." He paused. "But as long as you keep your mouth shut and don't do anything suspicious, everything will be fine. And everyone will *live*," he added pointedly. "It's in your hands."

And with that, the Cuban exited the bathroom, leaving Kevin with his hands clean and his head still spinning.

CHAPTER 21

"The real secret of magic lies in the performance."
—David Copperfield, Master Magician

Rachel felt numb and helpless, like a leaf swept up in a powerful river, not knowing where it was headed and not having any ability to resist its course in any event. Diego had told her approximately what she needed to say and the goal of the exercise—make sure she was taken along when Matt Gateway and his party left for the hospital. Lives depended on her ability to be convincing enough to make this happen.

She had had no idea what Diego was talking about at the time. After all, Matt was perfectly fine. But when he collapsed on the strip minutes later everything made horrible sense and she jumped into action, playing her role to perfection. She was sickened that harm had come to Matt Gateway and sickened further that she was forced to lie to his father. At the same time she was relieved that she had accomplished the twisted mission that had been thrust upon her.

She could not let the hostages down. Nothing else mattered. Everything in her life was finally going great, and she would not let Diego take that away from her. Her mother had managed to remain sober for the last two years. Rachel had beaten back the bullies that had tormented her. She excelled in school and had found a sport she loved. But more than this, she was an only child, and Kevin and Ben were like brothers to her now. Coach Bryant, in many ways, like a father. The thought of losing them was too much to bear. She would do whatever she had to do to make sure this didn't happen.

The group hastily boarded two cars parked beside each other and arrived at the base's hospital in a matter of minutes. A doctor and nurse met them out front with a gleaming, stainless steel gurney. The doctor wore a long white lab coat that almost touched the ground, while the nurse had a shorter lab coat, open to reveal blue scrubs underneath. Both were wearing white surgical masks that covered their faces from their chins to just below their eyes, and thin latex gloves.

Diego had told Rachel that this doctor and nurse were working for *him*, and to follow any instructions they gave her.

The bodyguard who was carrying Matt gently lowered him onto the gurney while Dr. Gateway made hasty introductions. "I'm Dr. Stuart Gateway, and this is my son Matt."

"Dr. Adam Green," said the doctor as he fitted a surgical mask over the boy's face. "This will reduce the risk to others if he's contagious," he explained, not wasting time shaking hands. He immediately shoved the wheeled gurney through the hospital doors. "This is Nurse Emory. I have a private room prepped and ready to go," he added, racing the gurney across the hard hospital floor so quickly Rachel almost had to run to keep up with him.

After the doctor had transported Matt fifty yards through the hospital in silence, he nodded at Rachel, not slowing his breakneck pace in the slightest. "Someone called a minute ago and said this girl has some insight into the patient's condition."

"That's correct," said Dr. Gateway as they arrived at the door to a private room and Dr. Green brought the gurney to a halt.

"Good," said Dr. Green. He removed a surgical mask from a shelf under the gurney and handed it to Rachel. "Put this on," he said. "The rest of you, wait out here."

"I'm staying with my son," insisted Dr. Gateway.

"I'm sorry, but I can't allow that right now. I understand you're worried about him," said the doctor sympathetically. "But he could be carrying a rare disease. We need to minimize contact with him until we know what we're up against. The nurse and I have to be with him. It's our job. This girl has already been exposed to whatever he has and has developed an immunity to it. We need to know everything she knows as soon as possible. She could prove instrumental in saving your son's life."

He opened the door and pushed the gurney inside. "No time to argue about it," he said firmly. As the door was swinging closed he added, "I'll give you an update in ten minutes."

Dr. Gateway fumed outside the door and began pacing nervously. He adored Matt and his expression reflected a fear and an anguish that only a parent with a child in jeopardy could know. The four bodyguards remained silent. They had developed affection and admiration for the young man themselves, but knew nothing they could say to his father could possibly help.

As soon as the door was closed Rachel turned to the doctor. "Is someone going to tell me why I'm really here?" she demanded.

She never got an answer. Instead, the nurse pulled a tranquilizer gun from under her lab coat and shot Rachel in the leg at point blank range. Rachel felt a sharp sting and began to crumple to the floor. The doctor caught her before she fully collapsed and laid her on the nearby bed.

He removed a large pair of stainless steel scissors from a black nylon duffel bag on the bed and immediately went to work cutting her hair. He sliced through handful after handful of it with the razor-sharp shears— cutting it off very close to her head. In only a few minutes time Rachel had been shorn like a sheep, and clumps of strawberry-blond hair now decorated the bed. Once the bulk of her hair was gone, the doctor took care to cut the rest to a uniform length—short even for a boy.

Before the doctor had even finished this task, the nurse removed a bottle of instant hair coloring from the bag. It was a carefully chosen shade of brown and could be applied directly to the hair. Rachel's hair was now so short the nurse was able to change it all to the desired color in record time.

The doctor and nurse completed their tasks silently and efficiently, having rehearsed every move dozens of times.

Once Rachel's hair makeover was complete, they removed her lamé and quickly dressed her in Matt's. They placed Matt on the hospital bed and carefully moved her onto the gurney, pulling a blanket over her legs and rear end. She was now lying face-down, her surgical mask still covering most of her face, and the words, "Gateway, USA" from Matt's vest displayed prominently on her back. Her short brown hair was now the precise cut and color of Matt's, and from behind her height and slight build were an exact match for his.

The nurse made sure Matt Gateway's body was out of sight on the bed and then threw open the door. The doctor drove the gurney forward like an unstoppable freight train, not pausing as he passed Stuart Gateway and the four bodyguards. "Follow me," he said urgently as he rushed by. "I think he'll be okay, but I need to run an important test in another room."

The five men hurried to keep up with the racing gurney, all of them gazing worriedly at the unconscious figure lying face-down on top of it. Not even Dr. Gateway suspected that this wasn't his son.

One alert guard had the presence of mind to realize Rachel was not with them. "Where's the girl?" he asked.

"Nurse Emory needs to ask her a few more questions," replied the doctor, not turning his head or making any move to slow down. "The nurse will make sure she's taken back to the tournament and is available in case any further questions arise."

"Do you know what happened to Matt?" asked Dr. Gateway.

"I think so, but I have to be sure," said the doctor. "But there isn't much time. I need to begin the diagnostic test." He arrived at the door to another room and stopped. He handed Dr. Gateway a surgical mask. "Put this on and I'll answer your questions while I work."

Dr. Gateway affixed the white mask to his face and started toward the door.

"We need to be present as well," said the head bodyguard firmly.

The doctor looked at Stuart Gateway with profound disapproval. "Who are these men?" he snapped. "Are they relatives of the boy?" He didn't wait for an answer. "I don't care who they are, they aren't coming in. This isn't a circus. I probably shouldn't even let *you* in, but I'm making an exception. I'll make sure they get updates."

Saying this, the doctor rushed through the door with the Gurney. Dr. Gateway caught the eye of his head bodyguard, Captain Drake Hanson. "It's okay, Drake," he said as he entered the room behind the doctor. "Wait here," he added as he closed the door.

Dr. Gateway began to walk toward the gurney but stopped short when he saw the .45 semiautomatic in Dr. Green's hand. "Say anything to alert your guards and the boy dies," whispered the doctor.

Dr. Gateway's face transformed from worry to anger as he adjusted to the new circumstances. "If you've done anything to hurt Matt," he hissed through clenched teeth, gesturing to the still figure on the gurney, "no power on Earth is going to save you."

The doctor glanced at the gurney and shook his head. "That isn't Matt."

"*What are you talking about?*"

The doctor rolled Rachel onto her back with one hand while keeping the gun trained on Stuart Gateway with the other. He lifted the surgical mask from her face.

Dr. Gateway's breath caught in his throat. It was the girl! The one who had been trying to help. She was unconscious. She was wearing Matt's lamé and her hair had been cut, but it was definitely her. They had pulled a switch.

"I can assure you that your boy is fine," said the man holding the gun.

"Are you even a doctor?" said Dr. Gateway in horror.

"No. And my partner isn't a nurse either."

"Who are you and what do you want?"

"I'm known as Rex. And the only thing you need to know is that my partner and I have killed on many occasions and won't hesitate to do so again. *Never forget that,*" he said chillingly, still not much louder than a whisper. "The moment we were out of sight of the other room, my partner loaded your son onto a wheelchair and brought him out to her car. By now they've already exited the base."

"How did you infiltrate the hospital?"

"Nellis hires a number of civilians to work here. We were hired three weeks ago as part of the night janitorial crew. The hard part was passing the background check." He frowned. "Not that mopping and cleaning toilets for three weeks is any picnic," he added irritably.

"But enough discussion," continued the mercenary. He pointed to a second door at the opposite end of the large room. "I'm going to put away my gun. If you ever want to see Matt alive again, you will quietly slip out this door with me and lead me to your car. We'll be passing through some crowded areas of the hospital, but don't get any smart ideas about escape. If the two of us aren't off this base in ten minutes," he said, shaking his head gravely, "not even I can save your son."

CHAPTER 22

"Hence to fight and conquer in all your battles is not supreme excellence; supreme excellence consists in breaking the enemy's resistance without fighting."

—Sun Tzu, *The Art of War*

Dr. Gateway didn't even consider resisting. Not when they had Matt. And he knew they did. They had snatched him from right under the noses of his father and four bodyguards.

The two men exited Nellis without a hitch. Once they had, Rex held his gun on his lap, pointed at Dr. Gateway as he drove his white Lexus sedan. "Get out your cell phone," instructed Rex, "and call your chief bodyguard, Drake Hanson." The mercenary went on to outline what Dr. Gateway needed to say. "For your sake and your son's sake, you had better be convincing," he added.

Dr. Gateway dialed and the phone was answered on the first ring. "How's Matt?" asked his chief of security worriedly upon picking it up.

"There's been a complication Drake," whispered Dr. Gateway, his voice thick with emotion. "They had to rush him into surgery."

"That's not possible," said Drake in confusion. "We've been standing near the door the entire time and no one ever came out."

Rex motioned for Dr. Gateway to take the next left and he nodded his understanding.

"The room has a back exit as well," explained Dr. Gateway. "It opens into a hallway that's closer to the surgical suites. We left that way. I've insisted on being present for the surgery. It'll take about five hours." He paused. "Drake, I appreciate your loyalty, but you and your men don't need to wait. I'll call you the moment we know something."

"If it's all the same to you, Dr. Gateway, we aren't going anywhere. Not when Matt is in trouble."

"Understood." There was a pause. "Thanks Drake. You're a good man. If you and your men will wait in the surgical waiting room I'll contact you as soon as I can after the surgery."

"What kind of surgery is it?" asked the bodyguard, deeply concerned.

"I've gotta go. The surgeon just finished scrubbing up. I'll see you in five or six hours and let you know how it went."

"Will Matt be okay?"

"They're almost positive they got him to surgery in time. Gotta go," he said, and ended the connection.

"Well done," said Rex happily as he snatched the cell phone from Dr. Gateway's hand. "You should have been an actor."

Five minutes later they entered the parking lot of a grocery store and Rex ordered Dr. Gateway to pull the car around to the back, behind two massive steel dumpsters that were painted green. Since no deliveries were being made the back of the store was presently deserted. A bright yellow minivan and a light blue Toyota Camry were also parked behind the dumpsters. Both were empty. Rex ordered Dr. Gateway to park the car next to the fencing van and get out.

Within thirty seconds a commercial van arrived and joined the two men behind the dumpsters, stopping with the vehicle's sliding door facing them. The woman who had called herself Nurse Emory was at the wheel.

The van was about the same size as Coach Bryant's van but didn't have a single window on the sides or back. *Ed's Heating and Air Conditioning* was painted on the side door, which immediately began sliding open to reveal Diego and Klaus standing side by side.

"Dr. Gateway," said Diego from just inside the van as he finished sliding the door open. "Welcome."

Klaus jumped down and joined Rex and his brilliant hostage on the pavement.

"It is indeed an honor," continued the Cuban. He extended a hand to help pull the scientist inside.

Dr. Gateway glared at him and stepped into the van, ignoring his hand. "Where's Matt?" he snapped.

Diego didn't answer. Instead he moved aside and gestured behind him. Matt was bound on the floor of the van, his back against the opposite door. He was still unconscious but breathing normally.

Just as Dr. Gateway began to move toward his son, Rex entered the van behind him and grabbed his arms, pulling them behind his back. He snapped a pair of handcuffs on him and spun him around, pushing him to a seated position next to his son. Klaus entered the van and slid the door shut behind them.

Rex bound Dr. Gateway further and taped his mouth shut.

"As you can see," said Diego pleasantly to Dr. Gateway as this was being accomplished, "your son is fine. The effects of the drug will wear off before too long and he'll wake up, good as new." A hint of a smile crossed his lips. "How long he stays this way is up to you."

The two arms dealers and Rex plopped down on the floor facing the two prisoners.

Klaus turned to Rex. "Any trouble?" he asked as the van began to pull away.

"None," said the mercenary. "I have to hand it to you two. You're as brilliant as advertised. To snatch such a valuable and heavily guarded target—and his son—from the most secure base in America is unbelievably impressive. But to do so without a single person realizing they're gone—not even their personal bodyguards—is nothing short of *spectacular*. Harry Houdini couldn't have pulled off a trick like that."

A smug smile came over Diego's face. "I trust Rachel Felder performed adequately?"

"Absolutely," he said with a chuckle. "Given that she was unconscious through most of her performance, she couldn't go wrong."

The three men didn't seem to care that Dr. Gateway could hear their every word.

"I can't argue with success," said Rex, becoming serious once more. "But as perfect as your plan was, it seems to me it could have broken down in any number of places. What would have happened if the Taylor boy had lost an early match? Or had won them all but still never had the chance to fence Matt Gateway?"

Diego laughed. "Never fear. We took every possibility into account. We had two backup plans, which I'm very glad to say we didn't need to use." He paused. "But to answer your question, Kevin Taylor wasn't the key at all. Rachel Felder was. Of them all, she was the only one who was truly indispensable. There were only three fencers entered in the entire tournament whose body types were a perfect match for Matt's. And for us to fool even the boy's father, the match *had* to be perfect."

Dr. Gateway glared at the three mercenaries with such intensity Klaus thought they might catch on fire. "Close those eyes or I'll close them for you!" hissed Klaus. Dr. Gateway gave him one last look of pure hatred and then complied.

"Rachel Felder was our first choice because she had a friend Matt's age who was an accomplished fencer," continued Diego. "And a coach I could impersonate without too much trouble. But that was all gravy. Having Kevin inject the Gateway boy during a bout was the least risky way to go, but there were other options."

"And if Rachel and her companions hadn't come to the tournament at all?"

This time Klaus answered. "We would have chosen one of the other two body-doubles we identified who were coming," he said. "We would have kidnapped *their* companions instead of Rachel's. We would surely have found a parent or coach that Diego or I would have been able to impersonate. Without a Kevin type, we would have had to go to a backup plan to inject the drug, but we would soon be in business once again."

"Truly remarkable," said Rex in sincere admiration.

"So far, so good," said Klaus as he hit a speed dial button on his cell phone. "But it's time to get things ready for the next phase." He paused as the phone was answered by the Korean mercenary. "Ahn," said Klaus into the receiver. "It's a go. We need the hostages out of the house."

He grinned at Stuart Gateway, whose eyes remained closed. "Time to make room for more important guests."

CHAPTER 23

"It [revenge] is sweeter far than flowing honey."

—Homer, *The Iliad*

Ben Chang, Ted Taylor and Coach Bryant had been handcuffed to the same wall for more than four hours. On the few occasions Diego had phoned, his men had ripped the tape from Mr. Taylor's mouth so he could speak with Kevin and convince him they were all still healthy. Then new tape would be applied and the prisoners would be completely ignored once again.

Ted Taylor knew their only hope was to escape and was confident the coach did also, despite the fact they could only communicate with their eyes. Kevin and Rachel were smart and resourceful. But as long as he and the others were hostages, the kids had no options. It was up to them to change this.

Finally, Ahn appeared along with a shorter Australian named Frankie. "Undo their cuffs," said Ahn, apparently in charge when the two arms dealers weren't around.

Ahn trained a gun on the hostages while Frankie unlocked their cuffs from the steel rungs set into the wall. He then re-cuffed each of the prisoners with their hands in front of them. A nine-inch chain between cuffs prevented them from spreading their arms apart, but after having had their hands immobilized behind them for hours this was quite a relief.

"Un-tape their mouths," ordered Ahn.

Frankie did so and he and Ahn led the hostages to the driveway outside, where a twenty-four-foot moving truck was now parked. It was white, with gray trim, and "U-Move-It" was painted in massive red letters on its sides. A ramp led from the pavement into the back of the truck, which was open and totally empty.

As they approached the back of the truck, Ahn rushed ahead, putting about ten yards between himself and the prisoners. He then turned and faced them with his gun drawn.

Frankie got behind the prisoners with his own gun drawn and gestured for them to walk up the ramp. Ted Taylor knew that if they were going to make a move, it was now or never. Kevin had told him several months earlier that the coach was also skilled in karate, so he knew that if he could create a diversion the coach might be able to take care of the rest. He caught Coach Bryant's eye and nodded, almost imperceptibly. The coach didn't know what was coming next, but he knew to be ready.

Mr. Taylor looked up at the sky and gasped, his face transforming into a mask of pure terror. Ahn and Frankie instinctively looked up for just an instant to see what had caused this reaction.

The coach attacked! He dropped to the ground and executed a low roundhouse kick. His leg traced a circular path behind him about six inches off the ground, sweeping Frankie's legs out from under him, and the mercenary crashed to the ground. Ted Taylor jumped behind the Australian the moment he was down and threw his hands over the mercenary's head, pulling back so the nine-inch chain between his cuffs pressed deeply into Frankie's neck. Using the chain, Mr. Taylor yanked him savagely up by the neck and onto his knees, crouching down behind the Australian to shield himself from Ahn's gun.

"Drop it or he's dead!" barked Mr. Taylor as Ben Chang dove for cover behind him.

Just after executing his kick, the coach had thrown himself into a roll, retrieving Frankie's gun where it had fallen and coming out of the roll with the weapon aimed straight at Ahn's heart. "Freeze!" he yelled at the same time Mr. Taylor was shouting his own threat.

Coach Bryant and Ahn each held their guns out in front of them with both hands, their arms fully extended and their guns trained squarely on each other. Neither man took their eyes off the other for an instant. Neither man even blinked.

"Drop it!" Ted Taylor demanded of Ahn once again, trying to break the stalemate. "I *will* kill him," he said, tightening the chain around Frankie's neck so it dug into his Adam's apple.

Ahn shrugged, his gun not wavering an inch from the coach's head. "Be my guest," he said casually. "If he's dead, there's more money for the rest of us."

Ted Taylor constricted the chain around the Australian's neck even tighter until gargling sounds emerged from his throat. Ahn completely ignored the strangling sounds being made by his associate. His focus on the coach didn't waver and he made no move to lower his gun.

Mr. Taylor abruptly stopped, and Frankie began coughing and gasping for breath.

"I didn't think you'd have the guts to do it," said Ahn with contempt. "Not that I would have cared. As for you," he said to the coach. "There's no silencer on the gun you're holding. So even if you could shoot me before I could fire—a very big if—the sound would alert every soldier in the house behind you. They'd come pouring out of it like ants from a kicked anthill." He raised his eyebrows. "And don't think you could escape in the truck. The ramp is down and the keys are inside the house." He paused and tried to look reasonable. "Surrender and I promise not to retaliate. It's your only chance."

The coach considered this for several long seconds. He glanced at Mr. Taylor who frowned deeply and nodded. Finally, with a deep sigh, the coach lowered his weapon and carefully placed it to the ground. At the same time Ted Taylor removed the chain from around Frankie's neck.

Frankie rose, slamming his elbow into Ted Taylor's face as he did so. Mr. Taylor reeled backwards and blood began running down the side of his face where the blow had landed and torn his skin. Frankie then aimed a vicious blow to Coach Bryant's nose, hoping to break it, but the coach's face wasn't there when his fist arrived. Given the coach could avoid being hit by an arm with a three-foot blade attached, he was easily able to dodge an arm with nothing but a four-inch fist on its end.

Frankie prepared to strike again.

"Enough!" thundered Ahn. He shook his head in disgust. "You were sloppy, Frankie. It's your fault, not theirs. You got what you deserved. Lock them in the truck."

The look of rage didn't leave Frankie's face but he stopped his attack. Ahn supervised as Frankie walked the prisoners up the ramp and into the truck. The Australian pushed them down hard against one wall. Soon their hands were cuffed behind them once again to metal rungs in the truck used by movers to tie down furniture. Without being told, Frankie decided to re-tape their mouths, making sure the heel of his hand slammed painfully into their faces as he did so. Each prisoner had already learned—the hard way—to roll their lips inside their mouths when the tape was being applied to protect them.

Satisfied that the prisoners weren't going anywhere, Ahn closed up the truck and he and Frankie reentered the house.

"Where's Dimitri already?" said the Korean impatiently to Frankie. "Go find him and tell him to get moving."

Five minutes later the truck pulled away from the house, with Dimitri at the wheel. The temperature was already stifling hot in the back of the truck and sweat began rolling down the faces of the prisoners. Mr. Taylor's unshaven face was now covered in grime, sweat, and blood. The back of the truck was as dark as a cave, and they had no idea where they were being taken or why. Each prisoner was alone with their fears and tortured thoughts.

Fifteen minutes later the truck stopped. The prisoners assumed they were at a red light until the back of the truck was rolled up, flooding the compartment with light. They squinted painfully until their eyes adjusted. Dimitri hopped up into the back of the truck. Behind him was nothing but untamed desert, stretching as far as they could see. "This is your lucky day," he said as he ripped the tape from their mouths yet again.

"Yeah. Real lucky," said Mr. Taylor sourly. "What are you going to do to us now?"

"Free you."

The coach eyed Dimitri suspiciously and Mr. Taylor shook his head in disbelief. There could be little doubt he intended to kill them here in the desert and leave them to rot. Perhaps freeing them beforehand was his sick idea of making more of a sport out of the slaughter.

Dimitri withdrew his gun and pressed it roughly against Mr. Taylor's forehead. "You look like you don't believe me," he hissed. "You think I'm lying, don't you? You think I'm gonna splatter your brains all over this truck."

Mr. Taylor was too paralyzed to speak.

"Answer me!" barked Dimitri menacingly, shoving the gun even harder against Mr. Taylor's forehead, enjoying his terrified expression.

"Aren't you?" croaked Mr. Taylor weakly, barely managing to get the words out.

"As a matter of fact," said Dimitri, relishing the absolute power he had over the prisoners, "no. But make no mistake," he continued, glaring at them with total contempt, "your lives mean *nothing* to me. Normally, I'd snuff you out without a second thought." He reluctantly removed the gun from Mr. Taylor's forehead and backed away. "But I need you alive. To be certain I get my revenge on Diego and Klaus," he finished icily.

"*What?*" whispered the coach in bewilderment.

Dimitri's lip curled up into a bitter sneer. "Those slimy sacks of puke were planning a double-cross," he hissed. "I'm new to the team and they don't trust me. They were whispering about it yesterday morning in their office. I heard every word through the air-conditioning vent in the upstairs room. *Double-cross me!*" screamed Dimitri. "They have no idea who they're dealing with!"

The prisoners glanced at each other and raised their eyebrows. The sound conducting properties of that particular air-conditioning vent continued to work to their advantage.

Dimitri walked over to Ben, still fuming. Ben cringed as the mercenary crouched down beside him, but Dimitri did nothing more than reach behind the young fencer's back and free his hands. When he was finished, he handed Ben the keys to free his two adult companions. While Ben knelt down to work on their handcuffs, Dimitri backed up until his shoulder blades pressed against the opposite wall of the truck and trained his gun on them once more.

"Their plan was to snatch a scientist and his son from Nellis," he continued, "and interrogate the scientist back at the house we just left. Once Diego grabbed them my job was to drive you around. Have Ted here call his son to tell him all was well so he wouldn't go for help." A bitter look came over Dimitri's face. "But they rigged this truck with explosives, timed to go off in a few hours." He pulled a small electronic device from his pocket with several clipped wires protruding from it. "The detonator," he said simply. "It was attached to a huge mass of C4 plastic explosive stuck to the bottom of the truck like chewing gum. They planned for *me* to be caught in the blast along with the three of you."

The mercenary's eyes blazed with hatred and his muscular arms tensed, causing the dark tattoos that covered them to undulate. "Well I've got a different plan!" he barked in fury. "They were gonna blow me up, so I'm gonna return the favor. I've rigged enough C4 plastic explosive in that house to blow it to Mars!" He glanced at his watch. "It's set to detonate in less than an hour. When Diego and Klaus and every last man working with them will be inside."

The expressions on the prisoners' faces turned from guardedly hopeful to panicked as they digested what he had said.

Dimitri laughed. "What's wrong?" he taunted. "You look worried. You thought I was gonna get revenge on Diego and Klaus by freeing you and ruining their plan, didn't you? And now you're wondering, if my plan for revenge is to actually *kill* these maggots, why would I need to set you free?" He paused. "Am I right?"

The prisoners remained silent, but it was clear from their expressions that he was.

Dimitri laughed again. "If you had any street smarts you'd see it. Think about it," he said with an air of superiority. "What if the timer doesn't work for some reason? What if the C4 is bad and the explosion doesn't happen? Or what if those puke bags don't make it to the house when they're supposed to?" He paused. "Well I'm not sticking around long enough to find out for sure. So if they do luck out and survive, you're my plan B. You and the kids can alert the military and help them capture these maggots. They'll rot in prison for the rest of their lives!" He paused. "A revenge almost as sweet as blowing them off the planet." The corners of Dimitri's mouth turned up into a cruel smile. "Almost," he added hatefully.

Ben had finished uncuffing the other two prisoners and was now in a standing position facing Dimitri. The mercenary waved his gun at the two men who were still sitting with their backs against the opposite wall of the truck. "Get up!" he ordered.

Ted Taylor and Coach Bryant raised themselves off the floor, keeping their eyes glued to Dimitri as they did so.

"Diego left the kids at the tournament," said Dimitri. "He's got a man on the base who'll be in place in a few hours. After Diego got what he needed from the scientist he was gonna have this assassin kill them both. Nice and clean. No evidence. No witnesses." Dimitri smiled. "But, like I just told you, I *want* witnesses. Just in case my plan fails."

Dimitri pulled a cell phone from his pocket and tossed it to Ted Taylor who snatched it from the air. "Your son's got a phone. Call him. Tell him you're free and clear so he can go to the authorities."

Mr. Taylor glanced up at the mercenary, and although he was trying hard to stay expressionless, he couldn't completely prevent the response that had come to his mind from showing on his face: *But we're not free and clear.*

Dimitri picked up on this just as surely as if the words had been spoken. Instead of reacting with anger, this time he just frowned. "What's the matter? Not an accurate enough statement for you? So what do *you* wanna tell him? That I told you I was about to release you, but you still aren't sure you believe me? No matter what happens with you, your son's life depends on him going to the authorities. Do you really want him to be worried about *you* right now?"

Mr. Taylor sighed. The mercenary was absolutely right. "No, of course not."

"I didn't think so," said Dimitri. He reached into his pocket, pulled out a laminated card with a phone number on it, and handed it to Ted Taylor, who quickly dialed and then shoved the card into his own pocket.

Kevin didn't answer until the fourth ring. The crowd noise was loud behind him, so his father shouted to be sure he would be heard. Kevin reported that he was fine and asked if they were okay, just as someone nearby bellowed something about a yellow card. Mr. Taylor ignored the interruption. "Everyone's fine," he replied to his son. "In fact we're free and clear. I repeat, we are free and clear."

Dimitri let them speak for only another thirty seconds before he extended his gun and barked, "Enough! End the call. Now!"

Mr. Taylor was irritated by this order, but this time was able to keep the irritation from showing on his face. He quickly told his son he loved him and tossed the phone back to the mercenary.

"Everybody out," ordered Dimitri.

The three San Diegans stepped from the truck into the endless desert. Large clusters of prickly pear cactuses were peppered randomly throughout the area. Each one looked as if dozens of green, elongated, Mickey Mouse ears—covered by two-inch thorns—had been shoved together haphazardly.

"Turn around, put your hands on your heads, and start marching," ordered Dimitri.

The prisoners didn't move. If Dimitri was lying, playing some kind of cruel game, this was nothing more than an execution. They put their hands on their heads and stared numbly at Dimitri, unable to bring themselves to turn their backs on this ruthless mercenary.

Dimitri fired! A bullet screamed from the barrel of his gun and grazed Mr. Taylor's left shoulder before he could even flinch, accompanied by a thunderous crack.

"Turn around, I said!" screamed Dimitri. *"Now!"*

Mr. Taylor's heart pounded so furiously it nearly exploded from his chest. A thin line of blood emerged from the shallow groove that had been sliced through the skin on top of his shoulder. If the shot had been six inches lower it would have killed him.

This time the prisoners were somehow able to force themselves to turn their backs on the mercenary, their legs so weak they could barely remain standing. The clusters of cactuses were the only cover in sight, and they would offer little protection from high caliber rounds. They stumbled forward, bracing themselves for a bullet between their shoulder blades; knowing that if one came it would bore a hole straight through them before the sound of the shot had even reached their ears.

"That's far enough," called out Dimitri when they had gone about ten yards. "Turn around."

The prisoners turned immediately, relieved to still be alive and at least facing Dimitri and the gun that was trained on them.

Dimitri closed the back of the truck and hopped into the driver's seat, his gun never wavering. He started the truck and lowered the window. "Civilization is four miles that way," he yelled over the engine, pointing south. "Diego and Klaus planned to kill you. But I wouldn't be surprised if you pathetic do-gooders still tried to save them. Even if the two hostages from Nellis *weren't* involved. But it won't matter. By the time you make it to a phone, you'll be too late. And you don't know the location of the house you were in anyway," he added.

"One last thing," bellowed Dimitri, glaring at them threateningly. "Don't tell the military what I look like or anything about me. If you do, I'll find out. And I'll hunt you down and make you wish you had never been born."

And with that, Dimitri put the truck in gear and began picking up speed, watching the three San Diegans recede in the rearview mirror with a malevolent sneer on his face.

CHAPTER 24

"Carry the battle to them. Don't let them bring it
to you. Put them on the defensive and don't ever
apologize for anything."

—Harry S. Truman, US President
Fenced in his Youth

The last thing Kevin wanted to do was fence. But withdrawing
from the semifinals would attract further attention to himself, and
Diego had warned him about that. The bout was scheduled to
begin in five minutes. He noticed several of the spectators pointing him out to others when they thought he wasn't looking. He
could guess exactly what they were saying: *There's the kid who
was fencing poor Matt Gateway when he collapsed* and *He really
doesn't deserve to be in the semifinals, you know.*

He wondered where Rachel was at that moment. Not knowing if she was okay only added to his almost unbearable level of
anxiety.

And then Major General Ronald Alexander entered the building in full dress uniform. He was an imposing figure, well over
six feet tall, without an ounce of fat on his body. He had been an
All-American fencer in his youth and he still fenced as often as he
could. He had white hair and a strong chin, and so many medals
and ribbons covering his uniform it was a wonder their weight

didn't crush him. He was light on his feet and his movements were effortless. Not too bad for a man in his fifties.

The general was surrounded by five underlings, and everyone who wasn't caught up in a bout turned to watch him. There were thousands of military personal based at Nellis and General Alexander was at the very top of the pyramid.

The general and his underlings walked purposefully through the gym and stopped in front of the strip on which Kevin was about to fence. The general was going to watch the semifinal match. Just perfect, thought Kevin in frustration. That was all he needed.

General Alexander and his men stood on one side of the strip while the rest of the large crowd gradually gravitated to the other side, spreading out along its entire length. The spectators apparently wanted to give the highly-decorated guest of honor plenty of room.

Kevin reluctantly took the strip against a kid named Greenblatt. Greenblatt liked to perform an aggressive fencing move called a fleche, pronounced *flesh*—the French word for arrow. When a fencer fleched he would leap explosively forward off his front foot and then instantly cross over with this back foot, attempting to impale his opponent as he shot forward. Unable to retreat after this explosive acceleration, the fleching fencer would race well past his foe like a sprinter, knowing that if his attack failed his only hope was to pass so quickly that he wouldn't get hit on the back as he darted by. It was a fun move to watch, and one that Kevin usually took advantage of. But not now. Greenblatt's fleches landed every time. Despite the large crowd, Kevin was in no mood to fence and quickly got behind four touches to one.

The phone Diego had given him rang by the side of the strip. It was the scheduled call from his father!

Kevin stopped fencing and was quickly stabbed in the stomach by his opponent as the phone continued to ring. The referee called the action and the new score as Kevin pulled off his mask and dashed to the phone.

"Hello," he said loudly to be heard over the crowd.

"Kevin, thank God!" shouted his father. "Are you okay?"

"Fine," said Kevin hurriedly, ignoring more than forty pairs of eyes now staring at him in astonishment. Fencers—especially fencers competing in the semis of a major tournament—did not just answer a phone in the middle of a bout. "What about you?" he asked anxiously, ignoring the referee in the background shouting, "Yellow Card, Taylor." He was being penalized for leaving the strip.

"Everyone's fine. In fact, we're free and clear," shouted his father. "I repeat, we are free and clear."

Kevin's heart raced. Could it be true? Was the nightmare really over?

"You have one second to put down that phone, Mr. Taylor," said the referee, "and come *on guard,* or I'll give you a Red Card."

"How?" said Kevin into the phone, so focused on his father he was unaware the ref had even spoken. "Are the mercenaries still a threat?"

"Red Card, Taylor," said the referee. "Point is awarded to Greenblatt. Greenblatt now leads six to one."

"Yes, they're still active, but you're in the clear. They have an assassin at the base who's supposed to come after you and Rachel, but he's not in place yet. Go to the authorities and tell them everything you know."

"Understood," said Kevin.

"I have to go now, Kev," said his father, his voice irritated at having to end the call. "I'll try to contact you as soon as I can. I love you, Son." With that the connection ended.

"Red Card, Taylor," announced the referee yet again. "Another point is awarded to Greenblatt. Greenblatt now leads seven to one."

A low roar erupted from the crowd as dozens of spectators began talking at once, unable to believe what they were seeing.

Kevin didn't care. He was elated. His father was no longer a hostage and sounded great. Ben and the coach were free also. If only he could be sure Rachel was okay this would have been the happiest moment of his life.

"Come *on guard* right now, Mr. Taylor," said the ref, "or you'll get a Black Card, disqualifying you from the tournament."

"That's okay," said Kevin. "I deserve it. I really apologize for all this, but I forfeit."

"You forfeit?" repeated the ref, shaking his head.

"Yes. I quit. Greenblatt wins."

This declaration caused a further uproar from the crowd. Kevin dropped his weapon roughly on the floor near his backup foil and waited about two minutes for the crowd around the strip to disburse so he was no longer the center of attention. It was the longest two minutes of his life. Finally, he rushed over to General Alexander who had remained near the strip, conversing with one of his men.

Kevin stared up at the imposing figure, impeccably clad in his full dress uniform. "General, I need to speak with you in private," he said urgently.

The general frowned. "I usually enjoy speaking with promising young fencers. But your conduct during this bout was very unsportsmanlike."

"I know, and I'm really sorry," said Kevin, "but there are more important things going on here right now. We have to hurry! This is a matter of national security."

"Sure," said the general dubiously, rolling his eyes. "National security." He shook his head in disgust. "Look, I'm afraid I have to go."

"I'm not making this up!" said Kevin in exasperation. "I was kidnapped by a team of mercenaries and brought here to fence. They've taken my father and two others hostage."

The general began to laugh and was about to say, "Are you sure you weren't kidnapped by aliens?" but quickly caught himself. The kid was as nutty as a fruitcake, but psychological problems were no laughing matter.

Even though Kevin was fourteen, and unarmed, the general and his underlings instinctively surrounded him, cutting him off from the crowd.

"What adults are here with you son?" asked the general with exaggerated calm.

"None," said Kevin in confusion. "I *told* you. They were both taken *hostage*."

The general nodded, now making an effort to keep his face as pleasant as possible. He gestured to one of his men. "Why don't you go with Lieutenant Jones here," he said in a strange tone of voice, as if talking to a sixyear-old. "He'll um . . . help us get to the bottom of this."

Kevin's eyes widened as he suddenly realized what was going on. "You think I'm *crazy*, don't you?" he bellowed accusingly.

The general made no reply.

Kevin took a deep breath and visibly fought to compose himself. As he settled down it occurred to him that his wild claims, coming out of the blue, *did* sound like the ravings of a mental patient. "Look, General, I don't blame you," he said as calmly as he could. "All of this seems crazy to me too. But it's all true. And it has something to do with Matt Gateway. He's in great danger!"

The general eyed Kevin with renewed interest. "I realize that, young man. He's in surgery even as we speak."

"This was the kid who was fencing Matt when he went down," pointed out Lieutenant Jones.

The hairs stood up on the back of General Alexander's neck. His intuition told him that it wasn't just coincidence that this mentally unstable boy just happened to be fencing Matt when he collapsed. "Is this true?" he asked Kevin.

Kevin nodded.

"Did you have anything to do with what happened to Matt?" he demanded.

Kevin shifted his eyes to the floor and a guilty look flashed over his face like a neon sign. He nodded miserably. "Yeah," he said. "But it wasn't my fault! I didn't know what I was doing. I was *forced* into it."

General Alexander glared at Kevin with enough intensity to melt lead. "Hold him!" he barked at Lieutenant Jones, who grabbed Kevin firmly by the arm.

Kevin couldn't believe he could be so stupid! If ever there was a time to lie, this had been it.

"What did you do to Matt?" hissed the general.

Kevin struggled to breathe, as if he had been punched in the stomach. "The mercenaries rigged my backup foil to inject something," he croaked, knowing he now had no other choice but to continue being honest. "Probably poison or a drug, I don't know. But he went down a few minutes after I hit him in the leg."

"General," said a captain beside him, "the kid's blaming imaginary mercenaries again. This must still be part of his fantasy world."

General Alexander shook his head. "Maybe. But maybe not. Even if he's crazy he might be telling the truth about what he did to Matt." He pursed his lips in thought. "Captain," he said pointing to Kevin's backup foil on the floor by the strip. "Test that foil and find out if what he says is true. If it is, get it to the hospital immediately and have them find out what Matt was injected with."

"Yes sir," said the captain, rushing off to carry out his orders.

"Lieutenant," said the general. "Get this kid out of here and find out if he has a history of mental illness. But no matter what—if he really did inject Matt—make sure he's interrogated immediately."

The lieutenant began pulling Kevin away from the general.

"*No!*" screamed Kevin. "*General, you have to listen to me!*"

Kevin's scream was loud enough to attract instant attention. Scores of fencers and spectators in the gym looked on in bewilderment, wondering what this outburst was all about and why a lieutenant was shoving a young fencer toward the nearest exit.

Kevin knew he had mere seconds to think of something that would convince the general he wasn't crazy or Diego and Klaus's plot—whatever it was—would succeed.

Kevin's heart skipped a beat. Perhaps that was it!

"*Diego and Klaus!*" he shouted in the direction of the general, who he could no longer see, as loudly as he could. "Those are the names of the mercenaries involved. Diego and Klaus."

Kevin held his breath. Would General Alexander be familiar with these two men?

The general's eyes widened. He motioned for the lieutenant to halt and strode rapidly over to Kevin. "Where did you hear those names?" he demanded.

"I told you. Those were the men who kidnapped us."

At that moment, Kevin had a sudden inspiration and realized what he should have told the general from the start. "They're after something called *Heaven's Shield*," he said grimly.

"And somehow, Gateway is the key."

CHAPTER 25

"When the sword is once drawn, the passions of
men observe no bounds of moderation."
—Alexander Hamilton, US Founding Father

The general's mouth fell open in shock, but he recovered almost instantly—coming to full alert as if he had been struck by a cattle prod. The boy wasn't so crazy, after all. He had known about Diego and Klaus. And the only way he could possibly have heard the name Heaven's Shield, or associated it with Gateway in any way, was if his bizarre story was true! Even the military personnel the general had brought to the gym knew nothing about this project.

"Lieutenant," said General Alexander hastily. "I'm leaving with this young man. Tell the others to remain here. I may or may not make it back in time to award medals. Apologize for me if I don't."

The general ignored the expression of stunned disbelief that came over the lieutenant's face and hurriedly led Kevin through the crowd—parting it like Moses at the Red Sea. Now, almost everyone in the gym who wasn't involved in a bout was watched this new development with their mouths open. This tournament was growing more bizarre by the second.

"Where are we going?" asked Kevin.

"To my staff car parked outside," replied the general. He pulled out a cell phone and hit a speed dial button. He was put through to the military head of the Heaven's Shield project, Colonel Elliot Gordon, even before they had reached the parking lot.

"Colonel, this is General Alexander. Change the command codes for Heaven's Shield immediately! Repeat, change command codes immediately. Authorization Alexander Alpha Niner Niner Delta Tango Charlie Zulu." He repeated the entire authorization again. "Do you copy?"

"Copy that, sir," said Colonel Gordon on the other end of the line. "Give me a moment," he added. Less than thirty seconds later he was back. "General, Heaven's Shield command codes have been successfully changed. I repeat, command codes have been successfully changed."

"Good work, Colonel. I want you to be on the highest alert until I tell you otherwise. Alexander out."

They reached the general's staff car, a large black sedan, and Kevin and the general slid into the backseat. The general pushed a button on the center console and a thick Plexiglas barrier slid slowly to the ceiling, creating a soundproof partition between the backseat and the general's personal driver.

"Tell me everything," said General Alexander anxiously the instant the barrier was in place. They made a strange pair—a young man in a white fencing uniform covered in sweat and a middle-aged general in his dress uniform covered in medals and ribbons.

"First check on Matt Gateway," insisted Kevin.

The general nodded and put in a call to Drake Hanson, Stuart Gateway's chief bodyguard. After a rushed conversation he turned to Kevin. "Matt's apparently still in surgery," he said.

Kevin didn't look convinced. "Can you have him make absolutely sure?"

General Alexander didn't hesitate. "Captain Hanson," he said, "I want you to get a visual confirmation on that. I don't care if you have to break down doors. Report back as soon as possible."

While they waited for Drake to get back to them, Kevin hurriedly told the general about the kidnapping and the conversation he had overheard between Diego and Klaus. Now that the general knew Kevin wasn't crazy, the boy was beginning to impress him. He could tell right away the kid was smart—and observant. While Kevin's summary was short and to the point, it was also thorough and captured many important details.

"You've obviously heard of these men before," said Kevin. "Who are they?"

"They're a pair of arms dealers, selling sophisticated weapons to enemies of the United States. We've been after them for years. We don't know their last names but they haven't changed first names in a while. Probably because we haven't gotten close enough for them to feel the need."

"What's Heaven's Shield?"

General Alexander frowned. "I'm afraid I can't tell you exactly. Suffice it to say it's a defensive capability."

"So what's with this Black Ops software and this *Devil's Sword* they were talking about?"

The general considered what to tell him and then quickly came to a decision. This boy had alerted him to an ongoing operation against them and deserved some answers. "I'm not sure," he said, shaking his head. "But if it's what I think it is, it's hugely troubling. The system is supposed to be defensive only. But there are rumors that an offensive version we thought had been destroyed still exists. That a rogue Black Ops group made a switch, and then created software that could turn the system into a weapon. Based on what you overheard, the rumors must be true. If they were able to get control of such a weapon they could bring this country to its knees."

Kevin's eyes widened in alarm, and he was about to reply when the general's phone rang.

"General, you were right!" said Captain Drake Hanson so loudly that Kevin could easily hear him from his position beside the general. "Matt isn't in surgery and neither is his father. We retraced all steps. They pulled a switch, General. The girl, Felder, was found in a room, unconscious. She was wearing Matt's fencing vest, with her hair cut and colored to match his. And she had a surgical mask covering most of her face. They fooled us, sir," he said miserably. "I take full responsibility."

The general cursed loudly. "Call up security and get footage of any car leaving the hospital around the time this switch took place. We're going to want archival and real-time satellite imagery on this one, so make sure you get it. If the satellite jockeys give you any trouble, tell them I'll take full responsibility. If they still give you trouble, tell them they'll be looking for new jobs on Monday. Understood?"

"Yes, sir," said Drake.

"Good. Also, activate Gateway's bug and transponder as soon as possible."

"Roger that. Is there a risk of losing Heaven's Shield, sir?" asked Drake.

"Not anymore," replied General Alexander. "Their plan broke down and we found out about it much sooner than they had expected. I changed the command codes. But they don't know that. There's no telling what they'll do to Dr. Gateway and his son."

Kevin waved his hands in front of the general until he had his attention. "Find out if Felder is okay," he whispered.

"What's the status on the girl who doubled for Matt?" said the general into the phone.

"Unconscious, sir, but otherwise unharmed. They're reviving her now."

"Good. Let her know that all of her companions are now safe, and have them bring her straight to helipad thirty-six as soon as possible."

The general closed the phone and turned to Kevin. "We'll find them," he said. "At the risk of giving even more classified information to a fourteen-year-old," he added, "there's a tiny bug and homing beacon under the skin in Dr. Gateway's upper thigh. These are normally dormant, but we're activating them now. We should know Gateway's exact location in a matter of seconds. Combined with satellite imagery, we'll get these guys. I promise."

Kevin nodded. Everything was coming together. With confirmation that Rachel was okay they had all come through unscathed. Still, something bothered him. An itch he couldn't scratch.

If the hostages were free, why had his father broken off the call so quickly? And why hadn't he called again?

Things had unraveled quickly for Diego. Almost too quickly. While Kevin despised the man, he couldn't help but admire his military genius. True, his plan was insanely complex, but he had managed to kidnap Gateway and his son without a hitch. It was hard to believe he had tripped so badly just short of the finish line.

On the other hand, no one was perfect. Not even Diego. He had made a mistake and he would soon face the consequences.

But there was something Diego had said that was troubling. Something about the words he had spoken to Kevin, just before he left the gym. Kevin's subconscious had already pieced it together, but his conscious mind hadn't quite made the leap.

But whatever it was, it was causing him to feel a vague uneasiness that he couldn't seem to shake.

CHAPTER 26

"Whoever saves one life, saves the entire world."
— Talmud (Collection of
Ancient Jewish Oral Laws)

Ted Taylor watched the large moving truck speed away. His face was covered in sweat and grime and blood, and he and his companions were now stranded in the middle of a desert.

He felt like dancing!

Kevin was going to be okay! They were *all* going to be okay. That morning he had pegged their chances of survival at less than five percent. They had been lucky rather than good, but that didn't matter. The nightmare was coming to an end. Even now Kevin was alerting the authorities to what was going on.

And there still might be time to save innocent lives from the fate that Dimitri had planned for Diego and his German partner. "We have to try to stop the explosion," he said urgently. "We can't let this scientist and his son die without doing everything we can to prevent it."

Coach Bryant nodded. "I agree," he said. He knew that even if they were able to warn Nellis about the danger immediately, without knowing the location of the house there was little chance the explosion could be stopped. But they had to *try*.

"Good. Let's move," said Mr. Taylor. He was in good condition for his age and the coach and Ben Chang were even fitter. "Dimitri said we're four miles from civilization. Let's hope this is accurate. Coach, if you can set a seven-minute-mile pace, I'll do everything in my power to keep up."

The three of them began running at a solid clip through the desert, trying to ignore the sweat that ran into their eyes and the throbbing of their temples from the intense heat of the midday sun. This was as fast a pace as Ted Taylor had ever run over this distance, and given the harsh conditions, he was in agony most of the way.

About twenty-five minutes later they could just make out a road and a gas station, with a convenience store on site, far off in the distance. After running for another four minutes they arrived.

Mr. Taylor burst into the convenience store and ran up to the attendant. "I need a cell phone," he said, doubled over and panting like a dog as he tried to regain his breath. "It's an emergency."

CHAPTER 27

"Nothing in life is so exhilarating as to be shot at without result."

—Winston Churchill

As the commander of the entire Air Force base, the general could make things happen quickly. Before he knew it, Kevin was on helipad thirty-six while commandoes readied themselves and two helicopters for imminent action. A jeep pulled up next to him and stopped.

Rachel Felder jumped out. Fully conscious and fully recovered.

Was she ever a sight for sore eyes, thought Kevin happily. She must have felt the same way because the moment she hit the ground she threw her arms around him. They hugged for the first time ever. Kevin's pulse quickened involuntarily as they did so, and he felt an electric tingle that startled him.

What was that all about? Rachel was a great friend, but he had never thought of her in any other way. But as they embraced, he suddenly wondered if he had harbored different feelings toward her. Feelings he had forced himself to ignore—terrified of the unpredictable ways this might change their friendship. No. He refused to even consider it. His reaction had been due to his immense relief that she was safe and nothing more.

When they parted, Kevin made a show of looking her up and down and then grinned broadly.

"What are you smiling about?" she said playfully.

"Nothing," he said wryly. "It's just that for a moment there, I thought I was hugging Matt Gateway." As he made the joke a tiny voice within noted that this couldn't be further from the truth, but he ignored it.

Rachel groaned. "Very funny," she said goodnaturedly. "But whatever you say, I know that I only look like Matt from *behind*. And only when I'm covered in several layers of fencing clothing."

"Okay," he said. "I'll give you that. I'm probably just reacting to the hair."

"What, you don't think army-length brown hair is a good look for me?"

Rachel knew her lack of hair would annoy her greatly for months and months to come. Right now, however, it was hard for her to be upset over losing her hair when she had been in real danger of losing her *life*.

Kevin had never admired her more than he did now. She could stay upbeat through almost anything, somehow finding a way to roll with every punch. "Well, let me put it this way," he teased. "The buzz-cut *does* make you look a little scary. But not much scarier than I'm used to seeing you," he added with a grin. "You know, wearing a dark steel mask and coming at me with a weapon."

Rachel laughed. "Good one, Kevin," she said, her eyes sparkling. "So how long are you going to tease me about this?"

"I'm done," said Kevin. "Promise. I really am sorry they did this to you. And besides," he said, "you're a lot tougher than I am. I saw where you kicked Wolf. I know better than to get on the bad side of someone with that kind of aim."

They were both still laughing several seconds later when the general approached them and directed them to board the chopper. One of the soldiers inside handed them each a sophisticated set of padded black headphones, with a speaker arm they could position under their mouths.

The two Pave Hawk helicopters lifted into the sky, their propellers slicing through the air noisily. The Pave Hawk was a modified version of the Black Hawk and had the same elongated body, like that of a dragonfly. It had room for a crew of four or five, including a pilot, co-pilot and gunner, and could carry eight to ten troops as well.

The helicopter had been modified for the Special Forces and had upgraded communications and navigation features along with significant computer capabilities. Colonel Gordon had just finished preparing a briefing. The general wanted to be in the air, and poised for action, while he listened to it.

Kevin and Rachel were with General Alexander, Colonel Gordon, and two Special Forces commandos, in full combat gear, in the front helicopter. Just behind, in the second, six additional commandoes were fully prepared for an imminent assault.

The colonel began his briefing the moment they were airborne. "We've activated the homing device imbedded just under the skin in Gateway's upper thigh," he began. The kids were impressed with how easily they could hear him through the headphones, which engulfed their ears and blocked out most of the roar of the chopper blades. "Dr. Gateway stopped moving about ten minutes ago," continued the colonel. "I'm pulling up a satellite image of his exact location." He pressed a key and a photo, clear as day, appeared on a forty-inch plasma screen bolted to one wall of the chopper.

"That's it!" shouted Rachel excitedly. "That's the house we were in."

Kevin nodded his agreement beside her.

"Good," said the general, happy to have confirmation they were on the right track. "What about the bug, Colonel?" he asked.

He shook his head. "It's been activated but we haven't heard anything yet. Since the homing device is stationary, Dr. Gateway could well be bound and gagged somewhere, or unconscious. In either case he's likely being left alone or the bug has malfunctioned."

"How likely is a malfunction?"

"More likely than you would hope, I'm afraid. The bug is quite small and delicate. And it has to be very sensitive to pick up sound while buried under several layers of skin." The colonel sighed. "Again, it may be working fine. It may just be quiet where Dr. Gateway is right now. In any event, if it ever does transmit anything it will be piped to our headsets. We'll hear it in real-time."

"Good," said the general. "Continue."

"The satellite experts went back and found imagery of Gateway's car after it left Nellis. At around the time the switch at the hospital was made."

The colonel brought up photographs of the white Lexus right after it had exited the base. The photos may have been taken from space, but few photographers could have captured a better image from even ten feet away.

"They traced the car to the back of a grocery store," he said, sending yet another picture to the forty-inch plasma screen. The car was now parked behind two green dumpsters along with a light blue sedan and a familiar yellow van.

"Very soon thereafter it was met by a commercial van," continued the colonel. He pulled up several pictures of the van, one after another. *Ed's Heating and Air Conditioning* was printed on its side. "We've checked. There is no such business in Las Vegas," he noted.

"The driver is the fake nurse from the hospital," said Rachel.

The colonel nodded and brought up the next shot. It showed two men standing just inside the sliding door of the van, which was wide open.

"Diego and Klaus," said Kevin firmly, identifying them.

"Rachel?" said the general.

She nodded. "That's them all right."

The next several shots included the fake doctor and Stuart Gateway. Diego had his arm extended toward Dr. Gateway in one shot, as if to help him into the van, and in the next Dr. Gateway was ignoring the outstretched hand and pulling himself inside. None of the satellite shots were able to show anything deeper inside the van.

The general frowned. "What about Matt Gateway?"

"He's already inside," replied the colonel. "The satellite experts also found the thread for the yellow van and the blue Toyota. We've been able to reconstruct everything. First, Diego drove the yellow van off the base and parked it behind the dumpsters. The *Ed's Heating and Air Conditioning* van was already parked there waiting for him. Later, the nurse imposter drove the blue Toyota with Matt Gateway inside. She met Diego and they loaded Matt's unconscious body into the *Ed's* van, after which she took the wheel. She then drove out of sight to await the arrival of her partner from the hospital and Dr. Gateway, which we just saw."

"So we've placed six people inside that van," said General Alexander. "The two Gateways, the doctor and nurse team from the hospital, and Diego and Klaus. Anyone else?"

The colonel shrugged. "Since the satellites can't see inside the van, it's impossible to say for sure. What we do know is that the van left the parking lot and went directly to the house I showed in the first photograph. It pulled into the garage. We weren't able to get any further imagery from inside the garage or house, of course." Another photo appeared on the monitor. "The satellite did show several men with automatic weapons checking the house's perimeter periodically and then returning back inside."

The general's eyes narrowed in thought. "You said Gateway hasn't moved in ten minutes. Hasn't moved a little or hasn't moved a lot?"

"Hasn't moved even a single inch."

"They may have drugged him," said Kevin. "We overheard them say they were going to try truth drugs on him first, although they expected this to fail. But Diego was still certain he could get the information he needed. He said he knew Dr. Gateway's weakness; his Achilles' heel. He must have been talking about Matt."

"No doubt they'll torture him ruthlessly in front of his father to get the command codes," said the general.

"It won't do them any good anymore," noted the colonel. "They've been changed."

"But they don't know that," said General Alexander grimly. He paused in thought. "What do you recommend, Colonel?"

Colonel Gordon considered. "We can be there in minutes. I recommend a frontal assault, shooting sleeping gas through the windows and picking them off if they try to leave the structure."

The general rubbed his chin in thought. A raid would put the Gateways in danger, but he couldn't see any better alternatives at the moment.

Kevin Taylor's cell phone rang. It was his father! Kevin slid his headset off and pressed the phone as hard as he could against his ear, straining to hear. The blades of the helicopter continued to make a horrible din as the pilots hovered in the air, awaiting further orders. "Dad, I'm in a helicopter. You'll have to shout."

"Diego and Klaus were planning a double-cross," said his father with great urgency, shouting so loudly he could be heard by everyone in or near the gas station convenience store from which he was calling. "They were going to kill Dimitri. He overheard it through the AC vent in the room you slept in. He set us free." He paused. "Did you get all that," he shouted.

"Got it," Kevin shouted back.

"To get revenge on Diego and Klaus, Dimitri has the house set to explode. It'll go off any minute. But Dimitri also said they're bringing two innocent people there. A scientist and his son. You have to warn the military. See if they can prevent this somehow. Hurry!"

"Hold on, Dad," said Kevin. He hastily repeated what his father had just said to the rest of the small group.

General Alexander was horrified by the news. The Gateways were in even more danger than he had feared. "Tell the pilots to get us to that house, best possible speed!" he barked at Colonel Gordon. The colonel switched channels on his headset and relayed the orders to the pilots.

The helicopter banked violently, changing course to make best speed to the mercenaries' headquarters. "We have to call and warn them," said General Alexander, ignoring the chopper's stomach-churning turn and descent. "Immediately. We don't have a choice. Colonel, can you get the number to the house's landline?"

"Yes, sir," he replied, his hands flying over the computer keyboard. "I should have it in a minute or two."

Ted Taylor was still on the line, waiting for Kevin to get back to him.

"You can speak with your father later," the general said to Kevin. "You and Rachel know these mercenaries and that house better than anyone. I need your full attention as we approach." He motioned for the nearest commando. "Captain, I'm going to have this boy give you his phone. I want you to speak with the man on the line. Find out where he is and send a chopper for him and his party immediately."

"Roger that, sir," said the commando, taking the phone Kevin held out to him.

"We'll be there in less than eight minutes, General," said Colonel Gordon intently.

CHAPTER 28

"We are going to have peace, even if we have to fight for it."

—Dwight D. Eisenhower, General, US President

Ted Taylor thanked the convenience store attendant for the use of the phone and convinced him to let him make one more call. When he and his two companions had first come into the store, filthy and battered looking, the attendant wasn't sure what to believe. But after overhearing Ted Taylor talk about double-crosses, being set free, and stopping explosions, he was beginning to think the emergency was real.

Before Mr. Taylor placed the call, he advised his companions to grab quart-sized bottles of water from the store's cooler and drink them inside the air-conditioned structure. They were all dangerously close to dehydration.

Mr. Taylor didn't say it, but he also knew that if they drank the water inside the store the attendant wouldn't immediately ask for payment. This was important since they didn't have a nickel between them.

They each began gulping down water eagerly, pausing only to breathe and to make sure they didn't get a cold-headache. Mr. Taylor finished one entire bottle and then opened another. While he was drinking his second he dialed his home phone number. No one answered. He tried his wife's cell phone with the same result.

He waited five minutes and tried again, relieved when she answered the call. "Jennifer," he said eagerly. "It's Ted."

"Where are you!" she shouted at him angrily. "Are Kevin and Ben okay?"

Mr. Taylor was taken aback. The night before he had told her they would call her around five o'clock to fill her in on the events of the day. Since this was still hours away, he had expected her to be blissfully unaware that anything was amiss. But this was clearly not the case.

"Yeah," he replied, wondering why she was specifically concerned about these two boys rather than the entire group. "They're okay. We're all going to be okay."

"Not if you don't explain what the heck is going on, you're not! The Changs called me thirty minutes ago in a panic. Ben said he would call them at noon from the tournament to let them know how he was doing. He never did. They tried to reach *him* but his cell phone was off. When they called the tournament around one o'clock to have him paged, they were told he had withdrawn due to illness. They called the motel to check on him, but he wasn't *there* either. None of you were."

Mr. Taylor could almost see the veins bulging in his wife's neck.

"Would it be too much to ask for you to call me when you suddenly have a major change of plans!" she said crossly. "Are you *sure* everyone is okay?"

"Yes. I'm sure."

"Then why did Ben withdraw? Why couldn't we reach any of you? Why did the tournament just tell me *you* didn't show up today at all and that Kevin withdrew in the middle of his semifinal match?"

"I can explain," began Ted Taylor helplessly.

"Well that would be nice, Ted," continued his wife before he could go on. "Considering Cameron and Dan have been calling hospitals in Vegas trying to find Ben for the past fifteen minutes. Considering that everyone is worried out of their minds and they're all on their way to our house to pool resources. Karen Felder will be here any second and the Changs in about twenty-five minutes. Everyone even agreed that we'd call the Vegas police if we couldn't locate you by dinner time."

She finally paused, but only long enough to take a quick breath. "You had better have a good explanation for all of this!"

"I do," said Mr. Taylor, but just as he said this a military helicopter swooped into view. Seconds later it was hovering over the gas station lot and dropping to the ground like a high-speed elevator.

"Jen, I'm going to have to call you back in a few minutes."

"What! You aren't going *anywhere* until you tell me what's going on!"

"I will," he replied. "But I have to sign off for a few minutes."

He didn't tell her he needed to borrow money from the pilot to pay for several quarts of bottled water. Or that he needed to return the cell phone he was using to its owner before borrowing another from the military. Why confuse her any further.

"I'll call you in a few minutes from the helicopter," he said. "I promise."

There was stunned silence on the other end of the line.

"Did you say *helicopter*?" sputtered Jennifer Taylor in disbelief as the connection ended.

CHAPTER 29

"You can't say civilization isn't advancing, however, for in every war they kill you in a new way."
—Will Rogers, American Writer, Humorist

The pilots brought the twin Pave Hawk helicopters to a low altitude and they swept past cars on the highway as if they were standing still. Before long they were racing over a sparsely populated area at speeds Kevin had thought impossible for this type of helicopter. The general had ordered *best speed* and the pilots were taking this order very seriously.

Suddenly the bug began picking up sound and sending it through everyone's headsets. It was working after all! All chatter in the helicopter ended in mid-sentence as everyone listened intently. First they heard the creak of a door opening. Faint but unmistakable. This was followed by the sound of the same door closing.

"How much longer?" said a voice impatiently, somewhat tinny and distorted.

"That's Klaus," said Rachel quickly. Despite the poor quality of the bug's reception she recognized the voice immediately. Kevin nodded his agreement beside her.

"He's regaining consciousness now, my friend. But he'll be pretty groggy for another ten minutes. Best to wait a little."

"Diego?" guessed the general.

Kevin and Rachel both nodded. Although this voice was even harder to make out, there was no doubt: it was a voice they would probably be hearing in their nightmares for years to come.

"This is a waste of time!" said Klaus anxiously. *"When Gateway is fully alert, let's just start torturing the kid. Nellis could discover the two of them aren't really in surgery and change the codes at any time."*

"It's worth another fifteen minutes just to be sure the drugs won't work. Their potency has improved over the last few years, so you never know. Besides, the boy probably won't be awake for another twenty minutes. And we need him awake for maximum impact. So his father can hear his screams."

A look of horror came over the faces of both Kevin and Rachel and they shook their heads in revulsion. Colonel Gordon had continued to work on finding the telephone number to the house and had finally succeeded. He handed the number to General Alexander who hastily dialed it.

"Leave Matt out of this," said Stuart Gateway, slowly and almost drunkenly. The bug had just as much trouble delivering his voice clearly, and his words were thick and slurred from the truth drugs he had been given. Still, his deep, gravelly voice was instantly recognizable.

They were now very near their destination. The mercenaries' headquarters appeared as a pinpoint in the distance, but grew with remarkable speed as the helicopters screamed over the desert, leaving a cloud of dust and loose sagebrush behind them. They were within a hundred yards. The bug picked up the sound of the phone ringing inside the house as the general's call went through.

"Pick up the phone," grumbled the general anxiously as it rang for the second time.

The house exploded into a massive fireball!

The roar of the explosion was deafening, like the sound of thunder amplified a hundred times. The fireball was immense, and would have blinded them all had they been any closer. The shock wave from the mighty explosion shook the helicopters and only the pilots' quick reflexes prevented them from crashing. Both helicopters pulled up, while all passengers stared in horror at the raging inferno that had moments before been a house.

Nothing could have survived such an explosion. Every living thing, down to the smallest bacteria and virus, had been consumed in an instant.

They were too late!

"Colonel," barked General Alexander, recovering from his shock. "Did the satellites show anyone leaving the house since the van arrived?"

The colonel frowned and shook his head. "No, sir. I'm afraid not."

Kevin and Rachel turned away from the distant wall of fire. A number of mercenaries had just lost their lives, but they couldn't bring themselves to mourn these ruthless men who had planned to kill them. Not at that moment.

But the terrible loss of Matt Gateway and his father left them both stunned.

The general ordered both helicopters to land about seventy-five yards from the still-raging fireball, choosing an area relatively free of sagebrush and other desert vegetation. Passengers, crew, and commandoes alike exited the craft and stared helplessly at the flames.

The few neighboring homes far off in the distance had been rocked as if an earthquake had struck. The residents were coming out to investigate, but were only visible as the tiniest of ants—if they were visible at all.

The general was interrupted from his trance with word that the pilot who had picked up the three civilians at the gas station had called for instructions. The general ordered the pilot to fly to his current location at best possible speed.

Kevin and Rachel had been through enough, he decided. The least he could do was hasten their reunion with their companions.

CHAPTER 30

"Trust your hunches. They're usually based on facts filed away just below the conscious level."

—Dr. Joyce Brothers, Psychologist

Kevin and Rachel stood beside General Alexander and gazed at the raging fire as if mesmerized, mourning the loss of a boy they had barely known but had already come to like and respect.

"How well did you know the Gateways?" said Rachel softly.

"Quite well," replied the general solemnly. "Stuart Gateway was brilliant, with a great sense of humor and a great sense of honor. A fine man. And Matt was something special. The nicest kid you'd ever want to meet. And very giving. He was always going out of his way to help new fencers learn the ropes."

Rachel and Kevin nodded sympathetically. The wind had picked up and several tumbleweeds the size of beanbag chairs rolled haphazardly across the desert.

"Your companions will be here in a few minutes," said the general woodenly, still devastated by the loss of Matt and his father. "I'll want to debrief all of you myself, but that will come later. Right now I need to speak with Colonel Gordon for a while before we head back to Nellis." He motioned for the colonel to join him and they walked about twenty yards away.

Five minutes later a smaller helicopter landed next to the Pave Hawks and Ted Taylor, Coach Bryant and Ben Chang jumped out the moment it did. They rushed over to Kevin and Rachel, who had been left to themselves, ten or twelve yards from the nearest commando.

Despite the recent loss of innocent life, the reunion was exuberant. The eyes of both Kevin and his father moistened as they hugged, and Rachel's eyes teared up as she embraced the coach. Ben was holding a cell phone to his ear, but lowered it to give Rachel and Kevin giant bear hugs; unexpected from someone known for being on the quiet and emotionally reserved side. Ben then put the phone back to his ear and continued speaking into it excitedly, wandering away from the group as he did so.

"Are you okay, Dad?" asked Kevin anxiously. It was impossible not to notice his father's bloodied face and shoulder.

"I'm fine. Don't let the blood fool you. I'll be good as new in no time." Mr. Taylor saw that neither his son nor Rachel were entirely convinced. "*Really*," he added with conviction.

The coach gave Kevin and Rachel a reassuring nod, indicating that Mr. Taylor was speaking the truth.

Kevin blew out a relieved breath. "So who is Ben talking to?" he asked his father. "His parents?"

"Yeah. Everyone back in San Diego has been worried sick about us. Apparently they all decided to gather at our house. When I called Mom from the helicopter, Karen Felder was already there, along with your brothers, of course. They put me on speakerphone so everyone could hear me. The Changs are still on the road, so I got off the phone fairly quickly so Ben could call them."

"So what did you tell everyone?"

"Just an abbreviated version of what happened— and that we had all made it through in great shape." Mr. Taylor paused and turned to Rachel. "You should know that your mother was in tears when she learned about the danger you were in," he said softly. "She asked me to relay a message. She said to tell you that she loves you very much, and she's going to dedicate herself to becoming the kind of mother someone as special as you deserves."

Rachel didn't respond, but several large tears emerged from the corners of her eyes and rolled slowly down her face.

"She said she'll tell you this herself, in person, in three hours or so."

Rachel shook her head in confusion, causing several tears to drop from her face to the parched desert floor. "I don't understand."

"She's planning to take the first plane to Vegas she can get on. She's coming to join us, Rachel."

Could it be true? Rachel thought. "But she hates to travel," she said in disbelief. "And she's terrified of planes."

Coach Bryant put his arm around her shoulder affectionately. "Maybe she's *more* terrified of how close she came to losing you," he said simply.

No one spoke for several long seconds. Rachel nodded and turned away, laughing and crying at the same time.

Finally, Mr. Taylor turned to his son. "Mom sends her love, of course. And although they didn't say it in those words, so do Daniel and Cameron."

Kevin's forehead wrinkled in confusion. "What do you mean by that?"

"Your brothers were just as worried about you as your mom was. I could hear it in their voices. Dan said that if you were hurt in any way he was coming after them himself. And he *meant* it."

Kevin's father paused in thought, trying to remember exactly what had been said. "Cameron told everyone he was sure you were okay," he continued. "He said that no one could handle themselves better in this kind of situation than you. That no one was any tougher, or any sharper. Dan agreed and said they had picked the wrong kid to mess with, and he had no doubt you would make them regret it."

Kevin was stunned. "Dan and Cam really said all that?"

His father nodded. "Every word. And they were pretty choked up when they did, too."

Kevin was speechless. Despite the occasional verbal brawl, he knew his brothers had come to respect him— and that deep down inside the three of them really did love each other. But as impossible as this had once seemed, Kevin suddenly knew in his heart that he and his brothers would end up being extremely close someday.

Ben ended his call and rejoined the group. Now that they were all together, the coach asked Kevin to brief them on everything that had happened while they were hostages at the house. Kevin did so as quickly as he could.

When he finished, the entire group fell silent, reflecting on all they had experienced. Emotions could not have run higher. Everyone was euphoric at having survived the ordeal, and touched and gratified by the support and love of those back home. This was especially true for Kevin and Rachel, for whom this love came from unexpected parties or was demonstrated in unexpected ways. At the same time everyone was deeply saddened by the deaths of Matt and his father and felt guilty to be alive and feeling so elated when these two good people had perished. These intense and conflicting emotions, constantly shifting like a spinning kaleidoscope, were as disorienting as they were exhilarating.

Kevin turned away from the seemingly inexhaustible wall of flames. "There must have been something more we could have done to save them," he said dejectedly as sadness and guilt once again broke through the euphoria.

Mr. Taylor shook his head. "Kevin, what happened is truly a tragedy. But we can't blame ourselves. We did everything we could. We're very lucky to have survived ourselves. If Dimitri hadn't overheard Diego's plans, they would have killed us all. And they would have tortured Matt and then killed him and his father when they had what they were after. You know they would have."

Kevin nodded. His father was right, but that didn't make what had happened any less tragic.

"You once shared a quote with me you said you liked," continued his father. He thought for a few seconds to get it straight in his head. "We shouldn't mourn that great men died, rather we should thank God that such men *lived*." He paused. "I don't remember who said it."

"Patton," said Kevin reflexively. It wasn't the exact quote but it was close enough. Kevin had taken the role of General Patton in his computer game many times. Patton had been an accomplished fencer, and Kevin knew more quotes by Patton than anyone else, other than perhaps Sun Tzu.

An electric jolt raced up his spine.

Sun Tzu! The author of *The Art of War*.

This was what his subconscious mind had been trying to communicate to him. *The Art of War* was a 2,500-yearold book on military strategy and tactics that was still used today. Some military strategists swore by it; memorizing every word as though it were the bible.

At the gym Diego had said, "He who knows when he can fight and when he cannot will be victorious." At the time Kevin couldn't place the quote. But now his memory had returned to him, clear as day. It was Sun Tzu. And from what Kevin had seen of Diego, he had little doubt he was a devoted disciple of the Chinese strategist. That was what had been troubling him.

The Art of War could readily be summed up in three words. Deception. Deception. Deception. Sun Tzu believed military campaigns should never be what they seemed. *If you are near, make the enemy think you are far away,* Sun Tzu had written. *When able to attack, we must seem unable.* He would have loved what Diego and his partner had managed to orchestrate at the hospital. The artful way in which they had fooled everyone.

What if Diego and Klaus were doing it again?

Sun Tzu had also written, *Making no mistakes is what establishes the certainty of victory.* What if Diego and Klaus had made no mistakes, after all?

"Follow me," said Kevin excitedly and then rushed ahead to where the general and colonel were standing. Kevin's companions hurried to catch up, startled by the sudden change in his mood.

"General Alexander," called out Kevin as he neared him.

The general eyed him with just a hint of irritation. Major Generals who were conversing privately with colonels weren't used to being interrupted.

"Sorry to interrupt you," said Kevin. "But I think this might be important."

The colonel had been speaking and waited for General Alexander to put the kid in his place, but the opposite happened. "Hold on to your thought for a minute, Colonel," said the general. "Let's hear what he has to say."

Colonel Gordon bristled. The general was cutting him off to listen to a fourteen-year-old. The colonel considered Kevin to be worthy of respect, but not *that much* respect.

"Thanks," said Kevin gratefully as his companions joined them.

The general hastily shook hands with the three newcomers and thanked them for their efforts to save the Gateways. He then turned back to Kevin. "On second thought, Kevin, we really should be heading back to Nellis," he said. "You can tell us what's on your mind on the way."

CHAPTER 31

"All great men are gifted with intuition."
—Alexis Carrel, French Physician,
Winner of Nobel Prize in Medicine

The general signaled for the men to return to their helicopters. "You five are with me," he said to the five San Diego civilians.

Within minutes everyone was back in the helicopters and fitted with headsets, and the general was ready to hear what Kevin thought was so important.

"Diego and Klaus have a genius for deception," said Kevin into the small microphone near his chin as the helicopter began lifting into the air. "Their trick at the hospital is a great example. So what if they're deceiving us again?" he said.

The colonel shook his head. "Impossible," he said. "They were in the house when it blew. There's absolutely *no* doubt."

"And the guard at Nellis had no doubt the man driving through the gate this morning was Coach Bryant," said Kevin. "And Dr. Gateway had no doubt that it was his son lying on the gurney and not Rachel Felder."

"Go on," said the general, still skeptical but prepared to listen.

"Diego and Klaus planned this operation down to the last detail. They were unbelievably thorough. They were somehow able to get pictures of everyone who was coming to the tournament to find the right body-double for Matt. And when they chose Rachel, they studied her very carefully—and us. They even hired computer hackers to track us on the Internet." He paused. "The wig Diego used to help him impersonate Coach Bryant was perfect and must have been made well ahead of time. And the way they changed out the tip of my foil for a version with a hidden, retractable needle— one that could still pass inspection—was *incredible*. They must have spent weeks working with an engineer to design something like that."

"So they were very good and very well prepared," said the colonel impatiently. "So what's your point?"

"My point is that these aren't the type of men who make mistakes," said Kevin.

"Everyone makes mistakes," said the general.

"Maybe. But let's imagine for a moment that *they* didn't. That everything we thought was a mistake wasn't—it was a deception. They only wanted them to *look* like mistakes."

"I don't see where this is heading," said the general.

"I'm getting somewhere," said Kevin. "I promise."

The general looked deep into Kevin's green eyes and considered. "Go on," he said.

"So what was their first—supposed—mistake?" said Kevin.

"The air conditioning vent," said Rachel. "We could overhear their conversation."

"Okay," said Kevin. "Let's supposed this wasn't a mistake. That they *knew* we would hear them. Let's even suppose they rigged the house to *make sure* we could hear them."

"But why? It makes no sense," said Ben.

"It does if they wanted to spread misinformation," said Kevin. "They made sure we heard they were serious about killing the hostages if we didn't cooperate. They made sure we knew their goal: prying the Heaven's Shield command codes from a key scientist."

"This last wasn't misinformation," said the colonel. "There's no doubt that this *was* their goal."

"Maybe," said Kevin, clearly unconvinced. "But let's move on for now. What was their next mistake?"

"The AC vent again," said his father. "Their *fatal* mistake. Dimitri overheard their plans to kill him and decided to set us free. Without that we'd all be dead."

"Again, let's assume this was all according to plan as well. That Diego and Klaus *wanted* you free. That it was all staged, and Dimitri was operating under their orders. They already made sure we knew about the vent so you wouldn't question Dimitri's story. Let's even assume for the moment that they *wanted* you to call me and tell me you were in the clear. So I would be free to go to the authorities."

"This is a waste of time!" snapped the colonel. "So they *wanted* us to change the command codes and foil their plan. Brilliant!" he said sarcastically.

Kevin ignored him. "What was their next mistake?"

There was silence for several long seconds. "Well, the military found the house they were using as a base almost immediately," pointed out his father. "For that to happen, the two of them must have done *something* wrong."

The general shook his head. "We activated a bug and homing device that were implanted in Dr. Gateway's thigh," he explained. "We found their base, but not because they made a mistake."

"But they did," said Kevin. "Their mistake in this case was not knowing about the bug and homing beacon. So again, let's assume there was no mistake. That they knew about these devices."

"Is that possible, Colonel?" said General Alexander.

The colonel nodded reluctantly. "Unlikely. But it is possible," he admitted.

"And if they *did* know about these devices," continued Kevin, "their plan would have taken them into account. Could they have removed them?"

The colonel frowned. "If someone knew they existed, and their location, they could be removed fairly readily," he said.

"So Diego and Klaus could have removed the bug and homing device from Dr. Gateway and had one of their men place them in the house to fool us," said Kevin. "So how can we be sure any of them were in the house when it exploded?"

"We heard all three of them through the bug just seconds before the explosion," noted the colonel. "Diego, Klaus, and Dr. Gateway."

"Are we sure?" said Kevin. "Diego and Klaus could have taped the entire discussion ahead of time. We could barely make out Dr. Gateway's voice and it was slurred. A halfway decent voice impersonator could have fooled us."

"It wasn't just the homing device and bug that placed him at the house," said the colonel. "The satellite footage did as well."

"Did you ever actually see who it was that entered the house?" said Kevin.

Colonel Gordon shook his head. "No. Again, the satellite shows the fake doctor and nurse, Diego and Klaus, and Stuart and Matt Gateway entering the *Ed's Heating and Air Conditioning* van. It then shows the van taking a direct, non-stop path to the house and pulling into the garage. No one got out of the van at any time. We're certain."

The general sighed and then shook his head. "Kevin, I'm impressed with how you're approaching this," he said. "Your logic is perfect—provided we accept the assumption that Diego and Klaus were perfect. But I don't. It's far more likely that these mistakes are what they appear to be—legitimate mistakes. We can speculate about anything. They *could* have been beamed to an alien spacecraft a second before the explosion for all we know. But the evidence we have is overwhelming that they were caught in the blast."

Kevin shook his head, discouraged. His every instinct told him his analysis was right. Diego and Klaus had set up their accomplices to die in the explosion, but *they* were still alive. They were fooling everyone yet again. He was confident he knew exactly how they had done it. All except for how they had managed to get out of the house unobserved.

"You're absolutely positive no one left the van on the way to the house," Kevin said to the colonel.

"Positive."

Kevin refused to give up. "Was the van ever out of view of the satellites, even for a few seconds?"

"No," said the colonel, shaking his head. But as he considered this further he thought better of his answer. "Not that I recall," he amended. "I'm almost certain it wasn't."

"You're *almost* certain, Colonel," thundered the general. "I need you to be a *thousand percent* certain! *Find out!*" he barked.

The group remained silent as the colonel's fingers once again flew over the keyboard. Three minutes later he looked up from the computer with a horrified expression. "Sir, the van was out of sight of the satellites for almost a full minute."

"When and where!" snapped the general.

"A small stretch of the road they were on ran under a major highway junction. They stopped for a red light under two crossing overpasses. The van was blocked from the satellites for fifty-three seconds. I'm putting video footage on the monitor."

The monitor showed the two overpasses and a traffic light beyond, just visible to the satellite. The van began braking long before it reached the light, even though it was still green.

The driver—the woman who had impersonated a nurse—had *wanted* to get caught by the light. She had slowed to be sure this happened. Sure enough, the light turned red and the van disappeared under the two intersecting overpasses, waiting with other cars for the light to change to green once again.

The general cursed. Kevin had been right! Diego and Klaus had brilliantly arranged to hide themselves from the watchful eyes of the satellites. And they had been fully prepared for this brief period of privacy, almost certainly leaving the van and switching vehicles. The entire operation had been executed to *perfection.* The footage of the van's journey looked so straightforward, so innocent, no one would have guessed in a million years that they weren't still in the van. No one but Kevin.

"I want footage of all traffic that emerged from under those overpasses after we lost sight of the van," barked the general. "All lanes in both directions. Over a period of about five minutes."

"Yes sir," said the colonel, getting to work immediately.

A few minutes later the colonel began transmitting photographs to the screen. As the general studied them he began to lose hope. There were dozens and dozens of vehicles. And the satellites couldn't see inside of them. By the time they traced all of them and determined who was inside, the two arms dealers would be long gone.

"Stop!" screamed Ted Taylor from beside the general. "Bring back that last picture."

Colonel Gordon did so. In the photo a truck was emerging from the underpass in the opposite direction the van was heading. *A twenty-four-foot moving truck with the words U-Move-It on its side.* The truck that Dimitri had been driving when he left them in the desert! Mr. Taylor was sure of it. He hastily explained its significance to the others.

"Call the NSA," said the general excitedly. "Have them pull satellite footage of this area from the archives. Tell them to get a thread on this truck and trace it after it emerged from under the overpass. If anyone left the vehicle at any time, I want the photos immediately."

They had arrived at Nellis and landed, but the general ordered everyone to hold tight. There was a chance they might soon need to race to a new destination.

Three minutes later the NSA transmitted several photographs to Colonel Gordon's computer. He pulled up the first one and sent it to the large plasma screen.

The photo showed the moving truck parked next to a deluxe motor home in an isolated patch of desert. Five people could be made out perfectly in the shot as they walked the short distance between vehicles. Dimitri was in the lead. Diego and Klaus were in the back, their guns trained on a familiar man carrying an unconscious boy wearing white fencing garb.

Stuart and Matt Gateway!

There was a collective gasp. Faces brightened all around.

They were alive!

They could still be rescued.

Just as Kevin had guessed, only the fake doctor and nurse from the hospital had been inside the *Ed's Heating and Air Conditioning* van when it had arrived at the house. They had brought the homing device and bug with them—removed from Dr. Gateway's body before he left the van—and had then played the recorded voices to fool the military into believing Diego, Klaus, and the Gateways where inside the house when it blew. The arms dealers must have given their associates some fictitious reason as to why this ruse was necessary—one that didn't involve their imminent demise.

The mercenaries had never suspected just how totally—and fatally—they had been double-crossed. They had carried out their orders to perfection—right up until the very instant the explosion had vaporized them and turned their headquarters into a fiery crater.

"Get a license plate number for that RV and have the NSA tell us where it is right this second," said the general. "And get both choppers in the air."

"Roger that, sir," said the colonel.

"Their plan would have worked," mused the general, having difficulty believing he had been played for such a sucker. "If not for Kevin's analysis, we would have bought their deception hook, line and sinker. Along with the data from our homing device, we would have taken the evidence from the satellite footage and their voices at the scene and accepted their deaths without question. We would never have examined the footage of the van's trip to the house from the perspective that they had deceived us. And we certainly wouldn't have done so immediately and in the presence of the only three people on Earth able to recognize their escape vehicle."

General Alexander shook his head in amazement. "Kevin was right in every regard," he continued. "Everything that happened, they *wanted* to happen. They *wanted* the kids to overhear that Heaven's Shield was their target—to be sure Kevin would get our full attention. Dimitri gave the hostages a logical reason why he wanted to blow the house—to get revenge on Diego and Klaus— so none of us would question it. They *wanted* us to activate the bug and homing device. Their timing was flawless. They made sure we had a front row seat for the explosion and undeniable evidence—evidence that *we* generated ourselves—that they were inside when it blew."

"I'm not sure I understand," said Mr. Taylor in confusion. "Even if we fell for their deception, what good would this have done them? They wouldn't have gotten what they were after, right? If I'm understanding this correctly, their plan would guarantee you would change the command codes, rendering any codes they forced out of Dr. Gateway useless."

The general shook his head grimly. "Their plan was never about getting the codes. Kevin was right about this as well. Everything they let the kids overhear was for the purpose of deceiving us." He frowned deeply. "Because even without the codes, their plan would have enabled them to bring America to its knees in just a few years time."

CHAPTER 32

"The sword is the axis of the world and its power is absolute."

—Charles de Gualle, French General, Politician

The RV was forty feet long and top-of-the-line. It contained a bathroom, kitchen, dining area, living room and bedroom. Two tan leather couches ran along the middle of the vehicle, facing each other, leaving about four feet of space between them.

Stuart Gateway and his son sat on one of the couches, handcuffed to a steel bar Diego had installed. Matt had awoken several minutes earlier. A bloodstained white bandage was wrapped around Dr. Gateway's upper thigh where Diego had removed the bug and homing device.

Klaus removed a bottle of champagne that had been chilling inside a stainless steel ice-bucket on the kitchen table. He popped the cork and cheerfully filled two delicate champagne glasses for himself and his partner. He walked up to the front of the vehicle and poured another glass for Dimitri, who was driving.

"Dimitri," he said. "You've been loyal to us for years. If we ever decided to take on a third partner, you'd be the one."

"It's nice to have your *complete* trust," he said with a sly smile. The other mercenaries who had worked on the operation had not yet earned the complete trust of the two arms dealers and had paid for this with their lives.

Klaus returned to Diego and they merrily clinked their glasses together. "This was the Super Bowl of our profession and we won big," said Diego. "We took on the greatest challenge imaginable and we hit it out of the park."

Klaus shook his head. The Cuban was obviously not a big fan of American sports. He had used a baseball analogy to describe their victory rather than a football one, but he let it go. They both took a long sip from their glasses in celebration.

Diego reached over and ripped the tape from Stuart Gateway's mouth. "I don't suppose you'd like to join us, Dr. Gateway?" he said mockingly.

"I hope you choke on that!" spat Dr. Gateway bitterly. "And aren't you celebrating a little early. You don't have Heaven's Shield *yet*. For all you know Nellis has already discovered your little deception and the satellite command codes have been changed."

The two arms dealers just laughed. "First of all," said Diego, "Nellis *has* discovered you've been abducted. We made sure of that ourselves. But if not for our help, they would have remained in the dark for hours yet to come."

"I don't understand," said Dr. Gateway, blinking in confusion. "Why would you alert them?"

"Because taking control of Heaven's Shield was never our goal."

"What else could it be?"

"What else, indeed," said Klaus with a triumphant grin. "Our goal was the offensive version of your laser, Dr. Gateway. Are you aware that your prototype laser, the one with enough power to strike the Earth from space, was never destroyed?"

"You're insane."

"I don't think so, Doctor. The prototype laser is what was installed on the Heaven's Shield satellite, not the original. Members of your own military pulled a switch. A Black Operations group.

And they created software that would activate the modifications, turning Heaven's Shield into the world's most powerful weapon."

Dr. Gateway said nothing, but the look of nausea on his face was response enough.

"Ah," said Diego in delight. "So you *have* heard these rumors. Well I've got news for you: they aren't just rumors."

Dr. Gateway glared hatefully at the two arms dealers. "So what. Even if all of this is true, and even if you have the software, you would need control of the satellite to turn it into a weapon."

"You are correct," said Klaus. "But while we were sure to convince everyone otherwise, this was never our goal either."

"Well, to be accurate," added Diego. "This *was* our original goal. But we quickly realized it would be impossible. The software is even more heavily guarded than you are. Once it went missing your government would have instituted the largest manhunt in history to find us. And they would have stepped up security on Heaven's Shield ten-fold." Diego grinned icily. "So we decided to do the next best thing. Kidnap the only scientist in the world who knows the secret to the technology. The only man capable of directing the construction of another space-based laser weapon."

"It turns out we made a little deal with a militant faction of the Chinese government," continued Klaus. "And while in the minority, this faction is quite powerful and well connected, and able to operate in secret. Our deal was this: We give them you—along with your son for leverage—and they give us four billion dollars." Klaus chuckled. "We realize they got the better end of the deal," he said. "But somehow we'll find a way to get by on only two billion apiece—minus a few million for Dimitri, of course."

"You see, the Chinese have their own satellites," said Diego. "And their own laser scientists. Oh, they're not as brilliant as you are, Dr. Gateway," he said, shaking his head. "But they aren't stupid either. With your help they'll be able to recreate your work. And they'll have Matt to motivate you. Cooperate with them, help their scientists build the ultimate laser, and you and he live a life of luxury. But if you stubbornly refuse to cooperate, you get to watch them torture little Mattie to death in front of you. And even then," continued Diego, "they'll just turn to truth drugs and get what they want anyway."

Diego calmly took another sip of his champagne, savoring both his drink and the look of utter despair on the face of Stuart Gateway.

"Truth drugs wouldn't be their preference, of course," he continued. "It would take them a long time to break through your resistance and even longer for their scientists to fish complex scientific information from your drug-addled mind. But they would ultimately succeed in recreating your work." He shook his head in mock sympathy. "Unfortunately, repeated use of these drugs would eventually cause brain damage, but they'd be more than willing for you to pay this price."

Dr. Gateway fought to remain calm. He could not let them rattle him further. "You spoke of the largest manhunt in history," he said. "What do you think is happening now that Nellis knows you've kidnapped me? They'll realize the danger. They'll understand that if a government with satellite capabilities got their hands on me they could recreate my work." He shook his head in disdain. "Even as we speak, the vast resources of the entire U.S. military are being organized to find me."

The two arms dealers laughed even louder at this. "I think not, Dr. Gateway," said Diego with a malevolent smile. "You see, the military is absolutely convinced that we're dead. And you and Matt also. We arranged for them to see it with their own eyes," he continued smugly, very pleased with himself. "Well, at least to *think* they did. It was quite the magic trick. And aside from present company, everyone who had even the remotest knowledge of the real objective of this operation was ah . . . tragically blown up." His grin grew even wider at this.

Dr. Gateway's lip curled up in horror.

"So the entire military *won't* be looking for you," continued Diego. "In fact, no one will be. Ever. And your government won't have any idea that a rival government faction is building the ultimate weapon—with your unwilling assistance—until it's far too late. Their success in this endeavor will allow them to wrest full control of the Chinese government from the current leadership. And when this happens, the first thing they'll do with their newly built Devil's Sword will be to destroy *your* Heaven's Shield—so you'll never be able to activate its offensive capabilities. And just like that," he said, snapping his fingers, "they'll have the only space laser in existence and your country will no longer be the dominant power in the world."

Diego shook his head. "No, Dr. Gateway," he said with pretend sadness. "I'm afraid no one will be coming to rescue you and Matt, after all."

CHAPTER 33

"May God have mercy upon my enemies, because I won't."

—General George S. Patton

Real-time satellite surveillance of the mercenaries' RV was now being piped into the lead Pave Hawk helicopter. The mobile home was traveling over an old desert highway that didn't get much traffic. And it was traveling five miles per hour *below* the speed limit. Its occupants thought they had all the time in the world and the last thing they wanted was to get pulled over by the police for speeding.

General Alexander hastily arranged for the Las Vegas Police Department to put up a blockade on the road behind the RV once it was out of sight so no innocent motorists would be in its vicinity. They put up another roadblock twelve miles ahead of the vehicle to block all oncoming traffic from that point as well. Since the RV was traveling so slowly vehicles already nearby soon passed it and continued to pull away.

The two choppers swept in, one on each side of the two-lane highway, about eight miles ahead of the RV. Two sharpshooters clutching sniper rifles rappelled down to the ground from each helicopter. The four commandoes were dressed in desert camouflage and each wore an earpiece from which a tiny microphone extended. The instant their boots hit the ground the choppers darted away; out of sight of the road and out of earshot.

Each pair of commandoes on either side of the road spread out and dropped to the ground. They readied their rifles and waited patiently.

General Alexander had considered having his men shoot canisters of sleeping gas into the RV but had decided it wasn't worth the risk. The gas could be dangerous in close quarters, especially if too much of it was breathed in. While Dr. Gateway and his son would be exposed, the arms dealers might have gas masks and be able to hold their breath long enough to get to them. Also, they didn't know the location of the two hostages and didn't want to risk hitting them with a flying canister.

General Alexander scrambled a third Pave Hawk helicopter from Nellis that he planned to use to transport prisoners. It joined them less than five minutes later.

Just as it arrived, the general's voice came over the commandoes' earpieces. "Target is now one mile from your position and maintaining speed. The satellite shows all oncoming traffic that was on the road before we put up the roadblocks is well past the RV."

Now they wouldn't have to worry about any vehicles arriving in the vicinity of the ambush for as long as both roadblocks remained in place.

"When the RV is approximately ten yards from your position," continued the general, "I will give the order to fire. Do you copy?"

All four reported that they did, one after another, in a prearranged order.

"Good luck men," said the general. "Remember that two of our own are inside that RV, so we need to get this right."

A little over a minute later the general's voice returned. "Okay, gentlemen. They should be within visual range now and you should be tracking." There was a long pause as the general studied the satellite image of the RV. "Fire on my mark in five seconds. Five . . . four . . . three . . . two . . . one . . . MARK!"

Four shots were fired at the same instant and every tire on the RV turned into heavy rubber shrapnel, including both pairs of side-by-side tires in the back—each pair taken out by a single, high-powered round.

The mercenaries inside the RV didn't know what hit them!

One second they were driving happily along and the next they were in the center of a war zone. The thunderous bark of rifle fire and exploding tires assaulted their senses and they were nearly thrown off their feet as the RV lurched violently downward. The glass of champagne Diego was drinking slipped through his stunned fingers and crashed to the floor. Several seconds passed before his dazed mind registered what was happening. They had been discovered!

It couldn't be!

The prisoners' mouths had been taped shut once again, but once they recovered from the surprise of the attack their eyes sparkled excitedly. Just when they thought all hope was gone it had suddenly returned.

Dimitri wrestled the massive vehicle to a stop and rolled from the driver's seat onto the floor, knowing that if he could be seen through the windshield he could be targeted. He hurriedly joined his companions in the living quarters of the RV, staying low. "How is this possible?" he demanded through clenched teeth as he neared them.

Diego shook his head woodenly, still in shock. "It's not," he whispered.

The sound of helicopters could now be heard in the distance. A sound that was getting closer with alarming speed.

Klaus turned to Dimitri. "Did you see what hit us?"

"No."

"Of course not!" barked Diego. His keen mind had already put the pieces together. "And you didn't see any other cars on the road during the last few minutes, either, did you." It was not a question. "We were ambushed. They blocked off traffic and planted at least four men ahead of us to take out the tires. The helicopters retreated far enough away that we couldn't hear them. They're heading back now."

"Can we escape before the choppers arrive?" said Dimitri.

"Don't be an *idiot*! The soldiers who shot out the tires are out there waiting. Take one step outside and it will be your last."

Diego was seething. If he had been driving and suddenly noticed a total absence of traffic around them in both directions for several minutes, he would have known an ambush was imminent.

The roar of the choppers became deafening as they swooped down for a landing. As soon as they hit the ground their engines were cut, and their blades quickly slowed and then sputtered to a stop. All became quiet once again.

Dimitri risked a quick peek out a side window, taking in the scene and then pulling his head back immediately. "Three choppers have landed about twenty-five yards away. Six commandoes with automatic weapons have fanned out around us, about ten yards away. A colonel and general are with them."

"The gig is up," spat Klaus sourly. "We have to surrender before one of them gets an itchy trigger finger."

"*Surrender!*" thundered Diego in dismay. "Never! We have important hostages. They're not going to risk hitting them."

Dimitri shook his bald head. "Diego, they've beaten us. I don't know how, but they have. There is no way out. We can't escape this."

Diego's eyes burned with rage. "I'm not going *anywhere*," he said.

Klaus and Dimitri traded glances. "Well we *are*," said Klaus. "Staying inside this vehicle is suicide." He shook his head bitterly, still unable to believe what was happening. "I wish you luck Diego."

Diego fumed but said nothing. Let them go! he thought in a fog of fury. If they had no backbone, he didn't need them.

The two mercenaries exited the RV with their hands over their heads. As soon as they stepped away from the vehicle four soldiers surrounded them. In less than a minute they were frisked, handcuffed and hustled off to the Pave Hawk the general had scrambled from Nellis. At the general's orders, Colonel Gordon stayed with the prisoners on the helicopter while the soldiers quickly returned to their positions.

Inside the RV, Diego slammed the butt of an assault rifle into one of the rectangular windows on the side of the massive vehicle three or four times in quick succession. The sound of breaking glass filled the air. His fourth hammer-strike caused the entire smashed pane to fall from its frame and onto the road below.

Diego pitched the automatic rifle to the back of the vehicle and removed a pistol from his shoulder holster. He undid Matt Gateway's cuffs and yanked him off the couch. Matt's father looked on in horror and struggled with his cuffs, but to no avail.

"Stand with your face where the window used to be, looking out," ordered Diego, pressing the handgun into Matt's back. "If you move from this position, I *will* kill you instantly, is that clear. I'll still have your father as a hostage."

The tape prevented a verbal response but Matt nodded his head and did as he had been told.

General Alexander's breath caught in his throat as Matt's face appeared in the window opening, facing him. The boy looked strong and alert, a very good sign. Six commandoes flanked the general, and each had their weapon trained on the RV. Two of the commandoes had stayed inside the helicopter the San Diego civilians were in to protect them.

"Diego, this is Major General Ronald Alexander, Commander of Nellis Air Force Base. You've got no chance. Come out now with your hands up."

"I have a better idea," shouted Diego from somewhere behind Matt, well out of view. "Call off your men! Do it or the boy dies!"

"I'm afraid I can't do that."

"You have ten seconds," threatened Diego.

"You are considered a terrorist," said the general. "The United States government has a very strict policy against negotiating with terrorists. But I can promise you this," he growled with a feral intensity, "*kill the boy and you kill yourself!* Do this and no matter what else happens, you will *not* live out the day. Even if you later surrender."

"Wrong, general. It isn't the policy of the military to shoot someone who is surrendering, regardless of their previous crimes."

"Very true. But in this case, I assure you it will be *my* policy," said the general with chilling conviction. "I will shoot you myself in cold blood and without one iota of mercy, since you are deserving of none. If I have to go to jail for my actions, I am prepared to do so. But make no mistake, Diego," hissed General Alexander menacingly, "I *will* kill you if you harm either hostage."

Diego knew in his heart the general wasn't bluffing and was overcome by rage and frustration. *"This is impossible!"* he screamed. *"How can you even be here?* Our plan was executed to perfection. There's no way you could have figured it out!"

The general shook his head. "I didn't. You had everyone fooled. Everyone but Kevin Taylor."

"Kevin Taylor?" he repeated in confusion. *"No.* I don't believe it."

"Believe it. He's in the chopper behind me even as we speak."

"Have him come out," insisted Diego. "I want to speak with him."

The general fumed, *furious* with himself. How could he have been so incredibly *stupid* as to bring Kevin into the middle of this? "I'm afraid I can't allow that. I won't put another innocent person in harm's way."

"Have him show himself or I'll kill both hostages!" shouted Diego. "And yes, I do believe you'll kill me if I do. But that doesn't mean I won't carry out my threat. Better a quick death than life in prison or a slow wait for an executioner's bullet."

Diego's voice became filled with rage. "Now let me see Kevin Taylor!" he demanded.

CHAPTER 34

"You win battles by knowing the enemy's timing, and using a timing which the enemy does not expect."

—Miyamoto Musashi, 17th Century
Japanese Samurai Considered One of
History's Greatest Swordsmen

Kevin heard every shouted word from his position in the helicopter and his heart began to pound violently in his chest. Diego was unstable at best, and their discovery of his plan may have pushed him completely over the edge. Maybe he only wanted to speak with Kevin, but it was just as likely he wanted to put a bullet in his head. Kevin had a bad feeling that unless they found a way to shoot Diego without hitting Matt, this could only end in disaster.

But how? Diego would never show himself and provide a target while any solider remained armed. And even if he did, they would need to orchestrate the timing with Matt beforehand so he could move out of the way the instant before any shot was fired. Without perfect timing, Matt wouldn't stand a chance.

"I will not put Kevin in harm's way," repeated the general.

Kevin's mind raced, knowing they were sitting on a ticking time bomb. He had to think of something! But it was *impossible*. Not when Diego was using Matt as a human shield. Not when the general had no way to communicate instructions to Matt short of telepathy.

"You have ten seconds to produce Kevin Taylor, General," bellowed Diego. "This is not a bluff. Ten . . . nine . . ."

The commandoes, their weapons still trained on the RV, tensed and glanced worriedly at the general for orders. The general considered various options at a furious pace.

"Eight . . . Seven . . ."

Inside the helicopter, Kevin's eyes widened as the answer exploded all at once into his mind. In a blur of speed, and in a single fluid motion, he snatched a .45 from the belt of a commando standing next to him and jumped from the helicopter before the soldier could react. Kevin shoved the gun into the back of his fencing pants without pausing for an instant and raced toward the general. The two commandoes in the chopper considered going after him but realized it was too late.

". . . four . . . three . . . two . . ."

"Okay, Diego!" shouted Kevin at the top of his lungs as he ran. "It's Kevin Taylor. Here I am. What do you want?"

General Alexander shook his head in irritation, but couldn't help but be greatly relieved by the boy's actions. Nor could he help but admire Kevin's courage.

Like everyone else, Mr. Taylor was caught off guard when his son had exited the aircraft. But as soon as he realized what had happened he raced after him, joining him only seconds after Kevin reached the general. He immediately stood between Kevin and the RV to shield him from Diego.

His father was risking his own life to protect him, and had done so without hesitation. Kevin didn't have time to dwell upon it then, but this was a gesture he would never forget.

Kevin reached out and pulled his father so he was sideways to the RV and stood this way himself. The first lesson a fencer was given was to stand sideways to their opponents to make themselves less of a target. The same rule applied when facing a gunman. Diego could still hit them, but it would take a far better shot.

"So you're willing to put the boy in harm's way after all, I see," said Diego triumphantly. "Wise choice general. You just saved Matt's life."

"What do you want?" repeated Kevin.

"I want to know how you discovered our plan. I want to know where we went wrong."

"Will you let Matt and his father go if I tell you?" said Kevin.

"No. But I *guarantee* I'll kill them if you don't."

"Come on, Diego. Wasn't it you who told me, 'He who knows when he can fight and when he cannot will be victorious'? Well now is a time when *you* can't fight. What would Sun Tzu advise you to do in this situation?"

Kevin paused for a moment to allow Diego to consider what he had just said.

"He would advise you to surrender and live to fight another day," he continued. "That's what. And you know it. If you surrender now, you know these men won't kill you. You'll be captured and imprisoned. You might be executed, but not for a long time. So you can still get out of this. Bide your time. Escape. If anyone is smart enough to pull it off, it's you."

There was absolute silence throughout the gathering for more than five seconds. No one even breathed. During the silence, Kevin caught the general's eye and then glanced suggestively at the gun shoved into the back of his pants. *Follow my lead,* Kevin mouthed silently.

The general nodded, not having any idea what Kevin had in mind.

"Tell me how you figured it out and I'll consider surrendering," said Diego finally. "Because I'm *positive* I didn't make any mistakes"

"Yes you did," said Kevin. "*Everyone* makes mistakes." He strained his brain to its limits, knowing he would only have one chance to get this right. "Mine was, um . . . running behind our motel instead of into the street when your men first attacked us. Matt here is a great fencer, but his big mistake is that he always fleches whenever he sees a parry six. The general's mistake was falling for your—"

"Enough!" interrupted Diego. "I don't need to hear a list of every mistake ever made. *Get to the point!*" he thundered, "or young Mattie here dies and I'll use his father as my next shield."

Kevin barely heard him. He was staring at Matt with laser-like intensity and nodding. Matt stared back in confusion—his mouth still taped shut—wondering if Kevin had lost his mind. What Kevin had said, that his mistake was always fleching whenever he saw a parry six, was total nonsense. He *never* did that. And Kevin had executed any number of parry sixes when they were fencing each other so he *knew* this wasn't true.

Matt's eyes widened as Kevin's intent hit him with sledgehammer force. Kevin hadn't just been babbling mindlessly. It was a message! The fleche was perhaps the most explosive of all fencing moves, and a term Diego wouldn't know. Kevin was coordinating an attack! When Kevin moved his wrist in an arc from left to right—a parry six motion—he wanted Matt to dive away from the window at that precise instant.

Matt nodded back at Kevin, ever so slightly. Kevin glanced at the general who nodded as well. General Alexander had known what fleching was long before Kevin was born and had picked up on his meaning immediately.

"Okay, I'll get to the point," said Kevin. "The point is this: you were *too* good, Diego. That was your mistake," he said earnestly.

"That makes no sense."

"Yes it does. Sun Tzu also said, 'Even though you are competent, appear to be incompetent.' You didn't follow this advice at all. In fact, you made it a point to tell me you knew my Internet gaming identity. You wanted to impress me with your thoroughness. With the effort you had put into your plan. And you did. You impressed me *too* much."

Kevin paused. "That's why I didn't believe you could mess up so badly. Especially after you showed your genius for deception at the hospital. So I assumed that anything that looked like a mistake was really a deception," he continued. "I figured out your entire plan from there."

Diego frowned inside the RV and shook his head. The kid was right. His mistake was flaunting his preparation; of being too good at the start. But this still shouldn't have mattered. Only a strategist as gifted as he was could have started with this simple insight and unraveled the rest.

"Okay," said Kevin. "I've answered your question. So surrender like you agreed."

Diego laughed. "I told you I'd *consider* surrendering," he said. "Well I *have* considered it. And I've decided not to. Because as smart as you are, kid, I'm still a lot smarter. When the general said he didn't negotiate, he was bluffing. When he had you leave the helicopter so I wouldn't shoot Matt, he showed me that. He showed me he'll do what I tell him to prevent me from killing the hostages."

Actually, Kevin had made the decision to join the general on his own, but stooped low behind Matt as he was and unable to see out of the window, Diego didn't know that.

"So now we're going to do things *my* way," continued the Cuban. "Have all your men put down their weapons and retreat back behind the farthest helicopter, general."

General Alexander did not respond.

Still completely shielded behind Matt and below window level, Diego lifted his arm high enough for the general to see his gun and pressed it roughly into the side of Matt's head. He moved it just a few inches and pulled the trigger, sending a bullet tearing just over Matt's ear. The sound of the gunshot was incredibly loud, causing Matt to instinctively jerk his head sideways and deafening him for several seconds. Even so, Matt recovered quickly from the shock and continued to watch Kevin intently for a signal.

"Don't make me have to ask again, General!" bellowed Diego, quickly removing his gun arm from view once again.

"Do what he says," General Alexander instructed his men.

The commandoes looked at the general in astonishment, unable to believe he would let Diego dictate to him in this way.

"*Do it!*" he roared as he saw their hesitation.

The commandoes on either side carefully dropped their weapons to the desert floor and retreated behind the farthest of the three choppers, twenty-five yards away.

"Okay," said the general. "I've done as you asked."

"Drop *your* weapons as well, General."

The general dropped his belt and handgun to the ground. Diego could hear them land even from inside the RV. "Okay. I'm unarmed."

Diego rose just enough to peer over Matt's shoulder at the view beyond. Electricity coursed through him as he saw all the weapons on the ground and the commandoes dutifully crowded behind the helicopter. The general was following his every instruction.

"Let me see your hands, General," he said.

The general waved his hands in front of him, showing Diego they were empty. The top of the Cuban's head was the only part of his body General Alexander could see as Diego peered over Matt's shoulder. But this was enough for him to make an accurate guess as to the exact location of the rest of his body behind Matt and the wall of the RV.

"I'm afraid I'm going to need one of your helicopters," said Diego. "So first, I want everyone to retreat at least a hundred yards. Then—"

He never finished the sentence.

Kevin flicked his wrist in the smallest, least noticeable parry six motion he could manage. The instant he did so the general pulled the .45 from the back of Kevin's pants and fired, knowing as he brought up the gun that Matt was exceptionally fast and would be diving out of the way. Sure enough, upon seeing Kevin's signal Matt dived sideways, away from the window, just as the general pulled the trigger. He was still in the air when the bullet left the chamber. Diego reacted immediately to Matt's movement, diving out of the way himself, but he was a half-second behind.

This half-second delay was all the general needed.

The bullet tore through the side of the RV and into Diego's stomach just as he launched into his dive. When he landed, blood was pouring from the bullet-wound in his gut and he was unable to hold onto his gun. Matt recovered from his own dive and hastily kicked the gun away from him. Still bound and gagged, Dr. Gateway could do nothing but watch anxiously.

"Stay here!" the general ordered Kevin and his father before covering the distance to the RV like an Olympic sprinter. He raced into the RV and over to where Diego was lying on his back in the middle of the vehicle, and pointed his gun at him. Diego ignored him, pressing a section of his shirt over his wound to try to slow the loss of blood.

Matt tore the tape from his mouth as he rushed to the general's side. Diego wanted to glare at them as they stood over him, but the pain was so incredibly intense all he could do was grimace through clenched teeth. *How had they done it?* The general had been unarmed. And their timing had been precise to within less than a second.

"How?" rasped Diego, his voice weak.

"Kevin Taylor again," said the General. "When he spoke of Matt's mistake as a fencer, it was a code. He coordinated our movements."

A hatred arose within Diego that was even greater than his blinding pain. And even more than this, a will to live. He had unfinished business to take care of. And although he was very close to losing consciousness, he guessed the gunshot wound would not be fatal. He had no doubt the general would foolishly go to great lengths to keep him alive.

Kevin Taylor had used his knowledge of Sun Tzu to attempt to convince Diego to give himself up. He had challenged him to escape. Diego was certain the boy didn't believe for a second he really could—not from a maximum-security military prison.

But, somehow, he would do just that. He would prove the boy wrong. No matter how long it took. The first step was to make a full recovery. After that he would bide his time. Appear to cooperate. Become a model prisoner.

Right up until the time he sprang his escape.

And when he did, he would pay a little visit to Kevin Taylor and his friends. And then he would give them all a very painful— and very final—lesson in the art of revenge.

And with this final thought, despite the intense agony he was in, the corners of Diego's mouth turned up into a cruel, satisfied smile and he fell into unconsciousness.

CHAPTER 35

"The highest reward for a man's toil is not what
he gets for it, but what he becomes by it."

—John Ruskin, English Poet, Art Critic

Klaus and Dimitri were flown back to Nellis, to isolated holding cells where they would await interrogation. Diego had been taken directly to the base hospital and was undergoing surgery. It had been close for a while but he was now expected to survive.

The five visitors from San Diego were flown back as well in one of the two original Pave Hawks while the general accompanied Stuart and Matt Gateway in the other.

Ted Taylor, Coach Bryant, and the three *Excalibur* fencers sat in the general's large outer office, waiting for him and Colonel Gordon to finish a private meeting with Dr. Gateway and his son. The general's staff had shown the San Diegans to the bathrooms and waited patiently as they washed up at the sinks as best they could. The staff also ordered a large selection of food and drinks and made sure their guests were as comfortable as possible.

Finally, the group was left alone. At long last Ben had the chance to say something he had been dying to say for some time now. "Um . . . having a bad hair day, Rachel?" he said innocently.

Rachel leaned over and hit him in the arm.

The coach tried to fight back a smile but failed. "I really do feel for you, Rachel," he said in amusement. "But look on the bright side. You'll be lighter on your feet without all that hair weighing you down."

"Let me see if I've got this right," she said with a twinkle in her eye. "We get captured, endure life and death situations, battle war-hardened mercenaries—Kevin saves the country—and all we have to talk about is my hair?"

"Well, we've all been under incredible stress for a long while," noted Mr. Taylor. "It's nice to be able to laugh about something again."

Rachel rolled her eyes. "Glad I could help," she said wryly.

"So what do you think," said the coach to his students with a mischievous smile, changing the subject. "I was right when I told you that regional tournaments were even more exciting than local ones, wasn't I?"

Everyone groaned.

"You just forgot to mention that they're also a whole lot more *life-threatening*," said Kevin in amusement.

"Yeah," said Rachel. "And next time I enter an exciting regional fencing tournament like this one, I'm going to try something different—like actually doing some fencing."

"You can say that again," agreed Ben.

"Look on the bright side," said Mr. Taylor. "You may not have fenced, but how many other fencers can say they've flown in a Pave Hawk helicopter. And one traveling low over the desert at its top speed at that."

The door opened and Matt Gateway emerged, shutting the door behind him, leaving his father alone with General Alexander and the colonel. It was the first they had seen of him since Diego had been shot. He walked up to the group and shook hands all around. When he approached Rachel a strange look came over his face.

Kevin grinned impishly. "It's like looking in a mirror, isn't it Matt?" he said, unable to stop himself.

Everyone laughed except for Matt, who had been unconscious at the hospital and had never been updated as to how Rachel had been used to impersonate him. "I don't get it," he said.

"Inside joke," said Kevin, wanting to wait just a few more minutes before explaining what had happened.

Matt shrugged. "Okay," he said. He studied Rachel once again. "You're Rachel, right?" he said uncertainly.

"That's me," she replied cheerfully.

"Didn't you have longer hair the last time I saw you," he said. "And wasn't it more, um . . . reddish?"

The entire group laughed again at his confusion. Finally, Mr. Taylor gave him a brief summary of what had happened at the hospital. Matt examined Rachel's hair once again and shook his head. "Unbelievable," he said in dismay.

"If *you* think it's unbelievable, how do you think I feel?" said Rachel. She shook her head in pretend anger. "It's your fault, you know. If you had long, strawberry blond hair, Matt, they wouldn't have had to do this to me."

This time Matt joined in the laughter.

"By the way, I have something of yours," said Rachel, who promptly turned her back to him. Matt now found himself staring at the back of a familiar silver-gray vest that said, *Gateway USA.*

"Okay," he said. "Now I'm really starting to get weirded out."

Rachel removed the lamé and handed it to him. "I can't tell you how happy I am to return this to you."

Matt accepted the vest and then turned to Kevin. "It looks like I have you to thank for saving my life. Twice probably. You stopped our kidnappers from getting away with their plan and then stopped that psycho from shooting me." He shook his head in admiration. "Fleche when I see a parry six. That's brilliant. The general told me he thought so too. Now that's what I call *team* fencing."

Kevin beamed. "I'm just glad you and your father are okay," he said sincerely, trying to keep his head from swelling.

Matt grinned. "You know, this really causes a problem for me. We're the same age and we both love fencing. Which probably means we're gonna be fencing against each other many, many times over the years to come. But now it's going to be impossible for me to have my game face on when we do. I mean, when someone saves your life, it's a lot harder to enjoy beating up on them without mercy."

Kevin laughed. "Why do you think I saved you? That was my plan. Tomorrow I'm going to find out who won our event and try to save *his* life."

Matt laughed. He was about to reply when the door to the general's office opened and they were ushered inside. His office was large, but even so, fitting nine people inside was a bit tight. Extra chairs were hastily brought in from the outer office and soon everyone was seated.

The general turned first to Rachel. "I understand your mother will be landing at McCarran Airport in just a few hours," he said. "I'll plan on having a helicopter pilot meet her at the airport and fly her here immediately."

Rachel grinned as she imagined her mother's reaction to being met by a helicopter and having to actually board a craft that was even scarier to her than an airplane. Rachel had spoken with her mother on the trip back to Nellis and the conversation could not have gone better. Her mom had told her she was determined to take Rachel's example and begin to embrace life rather than fear it. She had already been working hard to change herself for the better, but the threat to Rachel's life had strengthened her resolve. What if her daughter hadn't made it? She would have been forever tormented, not only by the loss of her daughter, but by the fact she had failed to become the kind of mother Rachel deserved far sooner. Rachel's ordeal had brought home the importance of seizing every day and living it to its fullest— because there was no way to predict what tomorrow might bring, good *or* bad.

It would take some time, but Karen Felder promised Rachel she would see some dramatic changes in her mother. Beginning with conquering her fear of flying. And while Rachel had no doubt she meant it, she decided that getting on a plane to come to Vegas was a big enough step for her mother to take in one day. Asking her to fly in a helicopter as well would definitely be pushing it.

"Uh . . . thanks for the offer," said Rachel sincerely. "But I'm not sure my mom is really a helicopter person. Is there any way you could have someone bring her here by car instead?"

"Absolutely. I'll make sure it's taken care of."

Now that this had been settled, General Alexander cleared his throat and turned to address the five San Diego civilians. "I'll want to speak with each of you individually, and at length, later on," he began. "But that's not why you're here now. Right now I just want you all to know how sorry I am that you got dragged into all this. And that I can't thank you enough for helping to stop one of the biggest threats to the security of the United States we've ever faced." He paused and turned to Kevin. "Especially you, Kevin," he said. "And although you won't be getting any fencing medals, I will be awarding all five of you medals nonetheless." He leaned forward intently. "You will each receive the Air Force Civilian Award for Valor. With my thanks and gratitude."

The entire group was stunned. "Really?" said Rachel in dismay.

The general smiled. "Really," he said. "And I have to say, these medals are even harder to come by than fencing medals." He paused. "And Kevin, you'll be getting a second medal as well. I'll let you know which one after I've had my call with the president tomorrow. But rest assured, it will be a high honor. And a very well deserved one."

Kevin was momentarily stunned. It was hard to believe that only two years earlier he had been a brace-faced geek with little self-confidence and few friends, squirreling himself away in his room most of the time. This was all like some kind of impossible dream.

"Wow. Thanks," he said gratefully, feeling a little awkward to receive this kind of praise.

"From now on," said General Alexander, "if any of you ever enroll in this tournament again, you will be my honored guests on this base, staying at the finest VIP guest quarters available. You now have the commander of Nellis Air Force base forever in your debt. If there is anything I can ever do for you, don't even hesitate to ask."

Everyone was spellbound by the general's heartfelt words of friendship and gratitude. No one quite knew what to say.

Finally, Kevin broke the long silence. "Well, there is one thing you can do," he said hopefully. "You can tell us what's *really* going on in Area 51."

The general laughed. "Good try, Kevin," he said. "I only wish I could." He paused. "But I'll make you a deal. You save the country just one more time and I'll tell you everything. I swear it."

Kevin grinned. "Just one more time," he said with pretend bravado. "That's all I have to do?"

"That's all," said the general.

"I'll keep that in mind," said Kevin, raising his eyebrows. "I'll definitely keep that in mind."

Made in the USA
Las Vegas, NV
22 December 2020